1

MAY 17

CH

A CRIMINAL LOVE 3
Lovin' A Street King

A NOVEL BY

K.C. MILLS

Text LEOSULLIVAN to 22828 to join our mailing list!

To submit a manuscript for our review, email us at leosullivanpresents@gmail.com

Synopsis

Royal finally gets the chance to face off with his egg donor, and it doesn't end well. He makes a decision that permanently changes things for him. After their encounter, Royal realizes that life is short and he needs to get it together, so he finally decides to tell Lace how he really feels.

Karter is on the grind, trying to locate Los so that he can put an end to the street war that was started when he decided that he couldn't live without Mo, but Los somehow gets the upper hand, putting Mo in danger.

Kay and Lane are finally figuring things out after she decides to let Kay prove that he's the man of he dreams, but they face conflict when Kay decides that he's ready for a family and Lane fears that motherhood is not for her.

Things were good with Shine and Meka until his past catches up with him and Asia shows up at their house, dropping a bomb that may tear Meka and Shine apart for good, although Shine has his mind made up that he and Meka are forever.

King and Free finally welcome baby Imani into the world, but complications with her delivery have them both on edge. Once she arrive happy and healthy, things go back to normal, until King gets a call from prison that he definitely wasn't expecting.

Everyone assumed that things would finally get back to normal once they settled all of their street wars, but they quickly learn that family and relationship drama turns out to be far more stressful and intense than any street life they were ever faced with. The girls and the guys all have unbreakable bonds, but will their relationships survive as life happens without warning?

Acknowledgments:

I would just like to say Thank You to my family. I appreciate your patience in allowing me to spend hours lost in my characters. You guys keep me grounded and I don't know what I would do without you!

I love you guys!!

Authors Note:

I am truly amazed at how much these characters have come to life. I appreciate you loving them just as much as I do. Thank you for taking this journey with me and I hope that you will stay with me as I continue to grow. There is so much more to come!!

Much Love to everyone that has supported me and continues to do so!

Happy Reading!!

King

"Free, are you okay?" She didn't say a word as she stared down at Sandra's body, which had me shook.

"Free, did you hear me?" I picked up her gun and tossed it to Royal.

"I'm fine. What do we need to do?" Free asked as she looked down at Sandra.

"You sure you good?" I asked, a little shocked at her reaction. She had just shot Sandra, yet she was calm as hell and asking me what we needed to do.

"I said I'm fine, Dey." She turned towards me with a seriousness that let me know that she was good, so I dropped it.

"Jason and Lee are on their way so they can get her to the warehouse," Royal said.

He looked down at Sandra, who had a bullet wound somewhere in her side from the one shot that Free fired off to save her best friend. Free originally had the gun pointed at Sandra's head, but when I called her name, she lowered it and the bullet hit Sandra in the side.

"Lace, you and Free get in my truck. As soon as Jason and Lee get here, go to the house and wait."

"Nah, fuck that. This bitch tried to shoot me," Lace said just before she kicked Sandra clean in the face.

"Lace, chill the fuck out. I got this. Do what King said. We don't have time to fuck around. We're out in the open and anybody could be watching."

She stared at Royal for a minute, and I could see her mind working overtime, but she let it go and pulled the handle to my truck and got in.

"You good to drive?" I asked Free, who was still a little too calm for me.

"Dey, I fine. Give me your keys."

I handed Free my keys, pulled her into a hug and when I let her go, I kissed her on the forehead. She smiled, walked around to the driver's side of my truck, and got in. Free had just shot somebody, and she was acting like it was just another day.

"Yo, there's the van," Royal nodded his head, and then stepped out of the way so that Jason could park.

Other than a few moans from the pain of being shot, Sandra hadn't said a word. She just lay there holding her side, glaring at both of us. I knew this was about to get interesting, because Royal was beyond pissed and Sandra was holding steady.

"What the fuck is this shit?" Lee asked as soon as he saw Sandra on the ground. It was dark, but we were all at risk because the parking lot to Sage House could be seen from the street. Royal and I kept watching the entrance, trying to make sure that we didn't have an audience. Luckily, we were on the end farthest from the street.

"Long story, bruh. Just get her in the van and meet us on Industrial," Royal said.

"Industrial?" Jason asked, now standing beside us. "Why the fuck are we going way out there?"

"Just do that shit," I yelled, "and hurry the fuck up."

We didn't have time to have a discussion about what moves we were making and why. Jason just looked at me and shook his head before he and Lee grabbed Sandra and dragged her to the side of the van. They bound her hands and feet before Jason checked out her wound.

"She's bleeding a lot, but she should be good for a while."

"Aight cool. We'll meet you there," I said.

"Keep that bitch alive," Royal said with fire in his eyes.

"Who the fuck is she anyway?" Lee asked, looking back and forth from me to Royal.

"My mother," Royal said before he unlocked the door to his Charger and got in the driver's side. Jason and Lee both looked at me, trying to see if Royal was telling the truth, and the look on my face gave them confirmation.

11

"What the fuck, King?" Jason said.

"We'll talk, just get her there," I said.

Jason and Lee got in their van and backed out of the parking lot, while I walked to the driver's side of my truck and waited for Free let the window down.

"How is he?" Lace asked.

"I got him, he's good." She looked across at Royal, who had his head back with his eyes closed.

"Take care of my man, King."

"You already know, Lace." She was worried; I could see it all over her face. Even though she was the one who came close to losing her life, she knew that Royal was about to do something that could mentally fuck him up in a way that none of us could understand.

"I hope so," she said, staring at him again.

"Are you sure you're good?" I asked Free on last time.

"Please don't ask me that again. I'm fine. Now go do whatever you have to do, and I'll be at home waiting for you." I just shook my head. I guess Free had it in her after all. It just took something like this to bring it out of her.

"I love you."

"I love you too, Dey."

I tapped the top of the truck, moved out of the way, and watched as Free backed out of the spot she was in and pulled off. Shit was changing with Free, but in a good way.

"You good bruh?" I asked as soon as I was in the passenger seat of Royal's car.

Royal turned his head slightly to look at me before he sat up and started his car. It took him a minute before he finally answered.

"If I ever had any doubts about whether or not I could kill that bitch, they went away the second she pointed that gun at Lace. I swear on everything real, I won't think twice when I finally pull the trigger."

I didn't bother saying anything, because there was nothing else to say. We just took the 45-minute drive to Industrial, and neither of us said a word until we made it to the warehouse.

Jason and Lee were already there, so we both got out and made our way to the door. Once Royal and I were inside, we found Jason and Lee cleaning up the area where they had Sandra. She was bandaged up and secured to a metal folding chair, and her eyes were on us the second we walked through the door.

"I gave her some antibiotics to hold off on infection. I didn't know how long you were going to have her here," Jason said.

Royal laughed as he walked over and grabbed an empty chair from the table that was sitting in the room. He picked it up and moved towards Sandra, placing the chair down in front of her so that they were face to face.

He just sat there in front of her with no expression, without saying a word. They just stared at each other, and I could feel the tension building between the two of them. I could see the hate all over Sandra's face. She hated her son and that shit was crazy to me.

"You got something to say?" Sandra snapped. She glanced at me before she laid eyes on her son again. Royal didn't say a word. He kept his eyes locked on her, sitting there silently. I knew him, and he was thinking.

"So how do you know Sen?" I asked. She turned to look at me with the most hateful stare before she laughed.

"I did my research," she said "you were sloppy, King."

"Sloppy how?" I asked, curious about what she meant.

"I followed you the night you met her at the hotel. I didn't know who she was, but I found out after your guy put her in that cab and sent her on her way. She hates you. It didn't take much for me to convince her to help me."

"Where is she?" I asked.

"The hell if I know. Her little girlfriend is hiding her."

I looked at Sandra with raised eyebrows. "Girlfriend?"

"Oh King, you didn't know?" Sandra said with a smirk. "Your little Blasian was batting for both teams long before the two of you ever met. She and Emily are quite a cute couple, I must say. Shocked the hell out of me too when I found out."

You have got to be fucking kidding me. So Sen licked clits. It made sense now that I thought about it. She always had some chick around her that I thought she was a little too cozy with, and she spent more time in Silhouette than I did. I always assumed it was about being there for Kemi, but apparently she was taking care of business of her own.

I glanced at Royal again, who was still sitting there. He hadn't said a word; he just kept his eyes on Sandra, and that shit was making me nervous as hell because I had a feeling his ass was gonna just snap.

"What about you, sweetheart? Do you have any questions for your mom?" Sandra said with a smirk, now focused on Royal.

He turned his head slightly as his eyes met mine before he calmly stood up and, without notice, rocked the shit out of Sandra, causing her chair to fall backwards. He sat back down and just stared at her, so I walked over and lifted he chair

15

off the ground and when she was facing him again, she spit blood out of her mouth, which landed on his leg.

Royal's crazy ass just looked down at the spot, laughed, and then stared at her again. If I ever thought his ass was crazy, I truly believed it now, but he had a good reason to be. His mother was a lunatic. Sandra didn't know how to read his behavior either, because she looked at me as if she was trying to figure out what was going on.

"That's your son," I said with a smirk.

"He's Doley's bitch ass son," Sandra's eyes fell on Royal, who finally spoke up.

"If you let my father's name come out your mouth one more time, then I promise you it won't work out well for you. You're already gonna die, no doubt about that, but how you die is up to you," Royal said calmly

"Fuck you and your father, both of you can go to hell. Oh wait," she let out a small laugh. "He's already there. Shy made sure of that." Royal stood up and pulled his gun out of the back of his jeans and pointed it at her head before he finally lowered it to her heart.

"One shot to the heart and this shit is over, but I know that you don't have one," and without another word, his gun was centered on her forehead again, and he pulled the trigger.

Sandra's blood went everywhere, and Royal just turned and walked out the door. When I made it outside, Royal was already in his car so I walked over to Jason, who was leaning against his van smoking a blunt.

"We good in there" he asked when he saw me moving his way.

"Yeah, we're good."

"So you wanna tell me why one of you shot Royal's mom?"

"Long story short, she hasn't been his mother in a long time, if she ever was."

"I feel you. He good? That's some pretty heavy shit."

"Shit I don't know, but it's done so he's gonna to have to be."

"Aight, well we got this shit."

I dapped Jason and then got in with Royal. He looked at me, and then started the car and pulled off. He was quiet the entire trip, until we pulled up at my house.

"She could have died because of me," Royal said.

"But she didn't," I looked him right in the eye; my brother was hurting.

"But she could have, and I don't know what to do with that."

"What you do is go in there get Lace, take her home, and let this shit go. Lace is good, Royal. She was more worried about you than she was about herself. Hell, she was demanding that I take care of your ass before they left. She's good, Royal."

He laughed a little before he got out. I knew that it was going to take some time, but for now, all he needed to do was focus on Lace. Everything else was irrelevant.

Lace

We had been back at Royal's place for over an hour, and he really hadn't said much. He watched me as I moved around the house, but he was mostly quiet the entire time, so when I finished my shower and found him sitting on the edge of the bed, I stood in front of him in between his legs and ran my hands through his hair. He looked up at me with no expression before he grabbed me around the waist. He hugged me with the side of his face pressed against my stomach and sat there silently, holding onto me so tightly that I couldn't move if I wanted to.

When he finally let me go, he looked up at me as I climbed onto his lap, grabbing the side of his face until his lips met mine. When I pulled away, he pressed his forehead against mine and finally spoke.

"I fucked up Lace, and I'm sorry," he said.

"For what?" I asked.

"For everything."

"I don't blame you for anything," I said.

"It doesn't matter whether you blame me or not, this shit is on me."

"I'm good and you're good. so none of it matters."

His arms went behind my back and he pulled me into his chest, resting his chin on my shoulder.

19

"You can't leave me, Lace. I mean that shit, you can't."

"I'm not going anywhere. You already know that."

He stood and I wrapped my legs around his waist, until he lowered me on my back and positioned his body on top of mine. Royal just stared at me, and I couldn't read his mood. He had a look about him that I had never seen before. Royal had just killed his mother and it had to be weighing heavy on his mind, but he wasn't the type to let his emotions control him. Right now, he was so overloaded with God knows what type of feelings that they were forcing their way out of him, so all I could do was be there for him.

It was late and I couldn't sleep, because I knew that Royal couldn't sleep. I lay there in the dark in his arms and he held on so tight that I couldn't move. It was like he was afraid to let me go, but I didn't mind. I wanted to be right there with him; he needed me, and how ever he needed me, I was going to be there for him.

"I looked her right in the eyes and all I saw was hate. I had no emotional connection to her, and I don't understand how that was even possible. How can you not love your own child?"

"Some people just can't. I don't understand it and I don't think I ever will, but some people can't."

"I guess it doesn't really matter anymore." He kissed me on my shoulder before he tightened his grip on me, which allowed his body to relax. Before long I could tell he was asleep, so I closed my eyes and tried to do the same

"Lace, wake up baby girl," Royal said as he kissed the side of my face. I could feel a frown forming as I yanked the covers up over my head.

"Mmmm, what time is it?" I asked.

"Don't worry about all that. Just wake your ass up and get dressed," he said, and I could tell he was smiling. I knew his moods by heart, just by the sound of his voice. I yanked the covers off my head and tried to focus on him as he stood over me grinning.

"You better be glad I love your little ass, because you look beat the fuck up right now," he said as he leaned down beside me and tried to kiss me, but I punched him as hard as I could in the chest.

"Chill Tyson, I was just playing. You know you're shutting it down, even with all that shit around your eyes and that dried up drool on your mouth."

This time, I lifted my leg and kicked the shit out of him and my foot landed right in between his legs, causing him to double over and yell.

"The fuck you do that shit for!"

"Because it's too damn early for you to be aggregating the shit out of me like that."

Royal held on to himself, but kept his distance as he narrowed his eyes at me.

"Your little ass damn sure better be glad that I love you."

"You better watch it. That's that second time in less than five minutes that you told me you loved me. Keep it up and I might actually believe you," I said as I sat up and pulled my hair out of the ponytail that it was in.

"You should, because I do," he winked at me, and then left the room and the second he was in the hall way, I heard him yell.

"Now get your little ass up. We've got some shit to do today."

I just sat there staring at the door, trying to process what just happened. We had been together for damn near seven months now, and not once had he ever verbally expressed how he felt about me. I mean it, was clear that he cared but I also knew Royal, and he was still fucking around, so he never once told me that he cared, and he damn sure never told me that he loved me.

Hell, I had been there a long time ago but I didn't really talk about it because he didn't, but this fool just told me he loved me; in only a way that Royal could, but he said it. I couldn't help but smile. I didn't know what had changed, but oh well. I could live with it. When I heard Royal moving around in the bedroom, I stuck my head out the closet.

"Where we going?" I asked.

"Just get dressed."

He walked in the closet and pulled me against his body before he leaned down and kissed me on the neck, and then let me go. He left the closest and as I grabbed a pair of skinny jeans and got them on, I heard his phone going off. Royal had his back to me, so he didn't realize that I was behind him. I watched as he sent the call to voicemail, and then dropped the phone back in his pocket.

"Who was that?" I could tell my voice startled him, because I could see it all over his face when he turned my way.

"Nobody, hurry up. We've got shit to do." Royal moved towards me, kissed me on my neck, and then walked out the room.

I was sure it was one of his many bitches, but I decided not to let it ruin my day. I decided to let it go and finished getting dressed.

Not long after, we were both dressed and in his car, heading towards what looked like my apartment. Sure enough, he pulled into my complex and parked next to my unit. I turned to him with the look of confusion, but before I could say anything his phone rang again. He pulled it out of his pocket and looked at the screen like he wanted to murder someone, and then sent it to voice mail.

"Just answer that shit, Royal. She's gonna keep calling you back until you do," I rolled my eyes so hard I was surprised they didn't get stuck. He just looked at me and laughed before he got out, so I sat there and waited for him to come open my door, which he did.

"So you think that bitches blowing up your phone while you're with me is funny? And why the hell are we at my apartment?" I asked as I followed behind him, since he didn't feel the need to wait for me.

When he reached my door, he pulled out a set of keys, opened the door, and then stood there waiting on me.

"How do you even...you know what, never mind. Why are we here?"

Royal took out his gun and moved around from room to room before he ended in my bedroom, sat on the bed, and just stared at me.

His yellow ass was doing the most; first he had his phone blowing up with bitches, then his crazy ass brought me to my apartment, which by the way he had keys to that I didn't give him, and now he was sitting on my bed not saying shit, like he was a fucking mute.

"Dallas Royal Dole, why the fuck are we here?" I said, standing in the doorway of my bedroom with my arms folded tightly across my chest.

"Why the fuck are you calling me by my government name?" he asked, mugging me hard as hell.

Again his phone rang, so he pulled it out, looking annoyed. This time, I snatched it out of his hand and jetted out of my room. I made my way to the bathroom with him on my heels, but I managed to slam and lock the door.

"Lace, stop fucking playing and open the damn door before I shoot this bitch, and you know I'll do it, so open the fucking door." I looked down at his phone and saw the name Shea, and of course I answered.

"He's with his main right now, so he'll call you back bitch!" I yelled into the phone.

"Who the fuck are you, and why the hell are you answering Royal's phone?' the bitch had the never to ask.

I just laughed. "If you don't know who the fuck I am, then you must not even be a side bitch. You must be just be sucking his dick because, even his side bitches know who I am, but at least they know their place. Now stop calling his fucking phone. He's good for today. I've got him covered but who knows, maybe you can hit him off tomorrow."

I hung up on the bitch and then opened the door to find him leaning against the wall looking calm as ever. I handed him his phone and then tried to walk past him, but he caught my wrist, held onto it tight as hell, and then yanked me into my bedroom.

"Let me go, Royal. I don't want to look at your yellow ass right now, so call that bitch back and maybe you can chill with her today."

His crazy ass just laughed, but he was anything but happy; in fact, he looked like he was ready to shoot my ass. He shoved me down on the bed, but I tried to get up and when I did, he pushed me back again.

"Sit your little ass down now, and I'm not fucking playing with you Lace, so don't try me. I'm not in the mood."

I mugged him hard as hell before I tried to get up once more, but he shoved me back again, this time with a look that stopped me dead in my tracks.

"Sit the fuck, down," he said calmly, but in a way that let me know to obey his command, so I did but you best believe I was mad as hell, and he knew it. Again, his phone rang, but this time he answered.

"Shea, stop calling my fucking phone. Damn bitch, I knew you were a little slow but I know you heard my girl. I'm with her right now, so dead that shit. In fact, I was gonna handled this later but lose my fucking number. I don't give a fuck, I said lose my fucking number because if I pay you a visit, it will only be to make sure you understand this shit is over." He ended the call, unlocked his phone, and then tossed it to me.

"Call whoever you want in there. I'm done. I know I've been fucking around a lot, and I know that you peeped that shit but I'm done, and I put that on everything. So call whoever you want on my phone and tell them whatever the fuck you want. You're not my main anymore Lace, you're my only." He stared at me for a few minutes, but I didn't say a word and neither did he.

"So you think that this little show is supposed to make me feel better? You just admitted to me that you're still fucking around after all these months, and yeah I peeped that shit because I'm not stupid, but this little performance doesn't fix anything."

"You're so damn stubborn, I swear. I'm not like other niggas you've been with Lace, and you know that shit. I'm a little fucked up in the head, but I admit that shit. Hell, I just put a bullet in my mother last night, so I'm a little emotionally detached. I don't trust women. I never have because from what I've ever seen, all they're good for is fucking and being fucked, but that shit changed when I met you. I tried to separate that shit and just keep it physical, but it didn't work so here we are. When I said that I loved you, I meant that shit on everything, so get whatever you want out of this little ass shit, put it in a bag, and let's go so that we can get the fuck out of here. I'm hungry as fuck, and I told you we've got shit to do today."

I didn't move and I didn't say a word. If I ever thought his ass was unstable, I was absolutely sure in that moment. How do you tell someone that you've been cheating, you killed your mother, and you love them all in the same breath, and then expect them to be like fuck it let's roll then? I laughed a little, because his insensitive behind was serious as hell but couldn't see how absolutely insane his little confession was. All he knew was that he was confessing his love, and no matter how twisted his approach was, he was being honest. That was my Royal; take it or leave it, but he was as real as it gets. When I didn't respond, he looked at me serious as hell.

"Damn Lace, what the fuck are you sitting here for, did you hear anything I said?" I just shook my head and rolled my eyes. His crazy ass wasn't gonna change, and I didn't want him too. I just stood up and looked around my room.

"We can do this later, let's go eat," I said with a grin. Royal pulled me into a hug and held onto me like it would be the last time before he let go and smiled.

"Good, because I'd rather pay somebody to do this shit. I know your little ass was probably gon' try and make me help."

"Fuck that, you are. I don't want some stranger going through my stuff, Royal."

After we were in the car again and on our way to Sage House so that he could check on the restaurant and we could eat, I looked over at my man and smiled. He was focused on the road so he wasn't paying attention to me, but a few minutes later he spoke randomly without looking at me.

"There aren't many people in this world that I love or have ever loved, so I don't take that shit lightly. Don't ever fuck me over, Lace." He glanced at me, and the look in his eyes was almost scary.

He reached over and grabbed my hand before lacing his fingers through mine, like he hadn't just threatened my life, but I wasn't afraid. I loved this man and would never turn against him or hurt him. If he didn't already know that, then he would find out in a matter of time.

King

"Dey wake." I could hear Free's voice and she sounded panicked, which immediately made me sit up and focus.

"What's up?"

Free was sitting up in bed, but she was leaning over with her arms wrapped around her stomach, which made me jump up.

"Something's wrong, Dey." I turned the light on and when I could finally see her face, she had tears in her eyes.

"What's wrong?"

"I just hurt. It's like a sharp pain in my side. Something's wrong, Dey."

I walked over to Free and kissed her on the forehead before I rushed into the closet. I threw on a pair of sweats, and grabbed a pair of Free Runs and a hoodie. When I was dressed, I walked back into the room.

"You think you can get dressed?"

Free nodded as I helped her off the bed, but the second her feet were on the floor she doubled over, falling into my body. That shit had me worried, because I could see the pain in her face. I picked her up and carried her to the leather chair that sat in our room, since the bed was so high off the ground.

"Free, you've gotta let me go baby, so I can get you dressed. We need to get to the hospital."

She slowly removed her arms from around my neck, and I made my way back to the closet and yanked one of her PINK sweat shirts of a hanger and grabbed her UGGs before I stopped at the dresser to get her a pair of leggings. After she was dressed, I kissed her on her forehead and rubbed her stomach. "I need to go wake Mira up." She nodded, but I could tell she was in pain.

I took off out of our room towards Mira's and when I got to her door, I just walked in. It was 3:00 in the morning, so I knew she was asleep.

"Mira, wake up baby girl. I need to take Free to the hospital." She mumbled something I couldn't understand before she opened her eyes and looked at me.

"What's wrong?" she asked as she sat up and tried to focus on me.

"Get dressed. I need to take Free to the hospital." Something clicked after I said Free and hospital, because she immediately climbed out of bed and began grabbing clothes

"Is it the baby?" she asked just before she pulled a sweatshirt over her head.

"I don't know, just meet me downstairs, and hurry up."

I left her room and went back to our room. When Free's eyes met mine, she had tears streaming down her face. I rushed to her, picked

31

her up, and started moving to the door. I met Mira in the hallway and she looked at me, worried.

"Go in our room, get Free's purse, my wallet, phone, and meet me downstairs. Hurry up."

She took off towards our room and I headed down the stairs, carrying Free in my arms. When I reached the last step, Mira was right behind me, and she rushed past me as me made our way through the kitchen towards the garage. She opened all the doors and I placed Free in the passenger seat of my truck. Mira climbed in the back, and we were on our way.

Free was quiet the entire ride. Her arms were wrapped around her body, and I could tell that she was in pain. My mind was all over the place. I needed her to be okay; I couldn't live without Free or Imani. Before all this happened, I never would have imaged loving anyone as much as I loved the two of them. Loving Mira was different. She was my sister so it was natural, but loving Free took time and effort. It snuck up on me and when I finally realized just how much she meant to me, I was in so deep that I couldn't see my life any other way. Now my baby girl was in the picture, and that type of love was something that I had no words for. I couldn't lose either one of them. That shit wasn't an option.

"What's going on, sir?" a nurse rushed to me as soon as I walked through the doors, likely because I had Free in my arms and she was crying uncontrollably.

"She's 8 months pregnant and woke up with sharp pains. She's still having them now."

The nurse waved her hand in the air, signaling for one of the other nurses, who approached with a wheelchair. I tried to place Free in it but, she was holding on to me so tight and wouldn't let me go.

"Baby, you have to let me go. They can't figure out what's wrong if you don't let me go," I said calmly, even though I was worried as fuck and about to lose it.

"Sir, I need to get some information from you." The nurse that had Free was kneeled beside Free asking her questions, while Mira stood next to them holding Free's purse in her arms tightly against her chest.

"Sir."

"Yeah." I turned to face the nurse, who looked at me with a soft expression.

"What's your name?"

"Kingston...Diego Kingston."

"Diego, she will be just fine, but I need some information so that we can take care of her, okay?"

"Yeah."

"You said she's eight months, has she already registered here with us?"

"Yeah, I think so. We did a tour a few weeks ago and she filled out a bunch of shit, sorry paperwork."

"It's fine, what's her name?"

"Free Evans?" I answered, but I kept my eyes on Free the entire time.

"Dr. Lennox?" she asked.

"Yeah."

"Okay, good. I have everything I need. Let's get her upstairs so that we can figure out what's going on. Lori, let's get Ms. Evans up to the fifth floor."

Lori, who I assumed was the woman with Free, turned and nodded as she began moving Free towards the elevator, with me and Mira right beside her. I let my hand run across Free's head and through her hair just before she grabbed it.

"I'm sacred, Dey. What if something's wrong with her?" Free looked up at me with tears in her eyes, which were flaming red. She was worried but hell, so was I.

"She's fine, Free." I needed her to believe what I said, even if I didn't

Thirty minutes later, Free was in a room and I was standing outside the door talking to Dr. Lennox, who insisted that we step outside to talk, which had me nervous as hell.

"She's about eight centimeters dilated, so we're having this baby tonight. It's early, but she should be fine. The problem is that her placenta is pulling away from her uterus and she hasn't fully dilated, so if she doesn't continue to progress then we're going to have to take the baby."

"The fuck you mean take the baby?" I didn't mean for it to come out like that, but fuck it. What she was saying sounding crazy, and I needed her to make that shit make sense to me. Dr. Lennox looked at me, but didn't seem moved by my words because she calmly began to explain.

"If she is not ready to push soon, then we're going to have to do a C-section and take the baby out. We'll do a small incision right at her bikini line, and then remove the baby. It's surgery, but not as bad as it sounds. We do hundreds every day, so I don't want you to worry."

I looked at her like she was fucking crazy. She was talking about cutting Free, taking my baby girl out, and then calling it surgery while telling me not to worry. This bitch had to be on some shit, but before I could respond, Lane and Kay came rushing down the hall.

"Where is she, what's going on?" Lane asked, looking at me and then Dr. Lennox.

"I don't know, talk to her," I said, frustrated as hell.

"I was just telling Diego that she's fine right now. But her placenta is pulling away from her uterus, so if she's not ready to push soon, then we're going to have to do a C-section. I don't want to wait it out and put the baby in danger."

"How long are you going to wait?" Lane asked.

"I'm about to check her now and see if she's dilated anymore. If not, we need to start prepping for surgery. I just wanted to let you know what was going on before we talk to Free, because her pressure is already high and I don't want her to panic."

"Are we clear on what's about to happen?" Dr. Lennox was now focused on me.

"Yeah we're clear, you just make sure nothing happens to either one of them, and I mean that shit," I said. Hell yeah, I was threatening her ass and I meant every word. My bullets didn't discriminate, so she damn sure better hope that both Free and my baby girl were good.

"King," Lane said, giving me a hard look because she knew I was threatening Dr. Lennox.

"Okay, let's go talk to Free but dad, I need you to calm down. If you're upset she's going to be upset, and we can't have that right now. This is about Free-are we clear on that?" I'll be damn if her ass wasn't low key threatening me now. I would have laughed if I wasn't so damn worried, because my threat didn't faze her. I guess she likely heard all kind of crazy shit in situations like this.

"I'll be out here. Royal and Lace are on their way."

"I'm her sister, can I go in?" Lane asked. Dr. Lennox looked at me, and I nodded.

"Okay that's it, just the two of you," she said.

"Where's Mira?" Kay asked, looking around.

"In the waiting room." I pointed in the direction where I left Mira and Kay nodded, kissed Lane, and then took off to go wait with Mira.

"What's wrong, what's going on?" Free asked the second we entered the room. She had calmed down some, but was still in pain and upset.

"This little girl has already got me up in the middle of the night. I can tell she's going to be trouble," Lane said as she moved to Free's side and brushed her hair out of her face.

"Free, I'm going to check to see if you're dilated anymore and if not, we're going to have to do a C-section. We talked about this being an option if things didn't go as planned. Do you remember that?" Dr. Lennox asked as she pulled on a pair of latex gloves.

"It's not time yet. I still have four weeks," Free said as she propped her feet up on the bed to allow Dr. Lennox to check her.

"It's a little early, but she'll be just fine."

I looked at my baby laying her in pain, her vanilla face looked flushed and tired as her eyes locked on me. I smiled, trying to ease her worry, but she was scared. I moved next to her and kissed her on the forehead and lips before she grabbed my hand and looked up at me.

"Free, do you feel pressure in your back or an urge to push?"

"It just hurts," Free said and the second she finished talking, she squeezed my hand, clenched her teeth, and tears rolled out her eyes.

"It hurts so bad, I feel like I can't breathe."

"Free, that was a contraction. You're ready to push. The next time you feel one, I need to you bear down and use everything you have to push."

"Push, what?" she tightened her grip on my hand again, and let out a light moan as her face balled up, and she closed her eyes.

"Free, you have to push sweet heart. When you feel that pressure, I need you to push."

Free shook her head and leaned towards me. "It hurts Dey, I can't do this."

"Baby, look at me. You can do this. Aren't you ready to meet Imani? You have to push, baby." I kissed her on the forehead again, just as another contraction hit. This shit was crazy, and I just wanted it to be over.

"Come on Free, you can do this, push Free," Lane said. She had one hand while I had the other.

Free tightened her grip, closed her eyes, and tried to push.

"Good job Free, she's coming. Try to relax and when the next contraction hits, give it everything you've got.

This bitch just told her to relax; whether Free was okay or not, I wanted to shoot her dumb ass for talking stupid.

"Okay Free, here we go. Push hard Free, you can do it." Free squeezed my hand so damn hard it felt like she broke my damn finger, and she let out the loudest scream ever and tried to push.

"You're almost there, Free. Her head's out. One more good push, and it's all over."

Free fell back on the bed, and I felt so helpless; she was drained and I couldn't handle seeing her like this, but before I had a chance to think about it, she was up again squeezing my hand.

"The last one Free, push hard."

"Come on Free, the last one you can do it," Lane said as her hand went across Free's forehead.

"Come on baby, last one," I said and then kissed her on the cheek as she pushed one last time as hard as she could, and then she collapsed against the bed again.

"Good job, Free. She's here. Your baby girl is just fine, she's beautiful."   I kissed free on

39

the lips and watched as Dr. Lennox handled Imani, who screamed at the top of her little lungs.

"Dad, you want to cut the cord?"

The look on my face must have been crazy as hell, because Lane laughed as Dr. Lennox handed me a pair of surgical scissors. I took them and she held up the cord for me, and when I cut it, I felt I was about to throw up. Here I was, a man that killed niggas daily without a second thought, but this shit had my stomach turning.

A group of nurses took my baby girl, cleaned her up and then handed her to me. I looked down at her and smiled. I was in love already. I walked over to Free and handed Imani to her. It took every bit of energy she had, but she held her tight and kissed her little face before she just stared at her ginning. I looked at my girls and knew that I would take the life of anyone who ever even possessed a thought about hurting them, and I put that on everything.

Free

"Damn, she's little as fuck," Royal said he as looked down at Imani, who was sleeping peacefully in Dey's arms. For somebody that swore he wasn't going to touch her until she was walking, he damn sure had her in his arms 24/7. She was going to be spoiled as hell, because Diego wouldn't put her down.

"Stop cussing at my baby, Royal," I said, and punched him in the arm before I walked up to Diego to take her from him. Royal and Dey were about to leave, and I needed to feed her and get her changed.

"I'm not cussing at her, I'm cussing about her, and she is little as fuck," Royal said with a big ass grin. I reached for Imani, but Diego turned his back so that I couldn't get her.

"Dey, please give me my baby so that I can feed her," I tried again, but he turned away from me once more.

"Chill with that shit Free, you can have her in a minute. She's chilling with her dad right now."

"Fine, then you stay home and feed her and I'll get back in the bed," I said

"Why are you up anyway? Isn't your ass supposed to be laid up for the next six weeks or something?" Royal said.

"No, dummy. I just had a baby, not major surgery. I'm fine, just a little sore."

41

"Shit, I can't tell, your ass don't even look like you had a damn baby," he turned to Diego. "You sure her ass wasn't lying and hiding a pillow or some shit like that under her shirt? Your ass is going to jail, King. Free kidnapped that baby."

"You're so damn stupid," Lace said as she walked in the room, hearing what Royal just said.

"How is that stupid? Does she look like she just had a damn baby?"

I pressed my hands against my shirt, showing the baby pouch I still had, but honestly most of my stomach was already gone.

"Hell yeah it does," I said.

"Here. We need to leave." Diego kissed Imani several times all over her tiny little face before he finally handed her to me. Once she was in my arms, he kissed me and then picked up his phone.

"I'll be late. Call me if you need anything. Lace, you staying?"

"Yeah, and Mo's on her way," Lace said, taking Imani from me. Damn, there was no hope; this child was going to be spoiled as hell.

"Aight, well make sure you set the alarm," Diego said.

"That's right, get comfortable with that shit because your ass is up next," Royal said before he kissed Lace on the neck and smacked her on the ass.

"You must be high. I told you that shit is not happening; your crazy ass is enough for me. I can only handle one child at a time," Lace said, and then rolled her eyes at Royal.

"I'm a grown ass man and trust me, I'm gonna remind you as soon as I get back, so be ready."

"Royal, take your ass on before you make me cuss you out." He just laughed, and Dey kissed me one last time before he and Royal left. An hour later, me Lace, and Mo were sitting in our living room, deep in conversation.

"So what's new at casa de Dole?" Lane asked, grinning at Meka.

"Insanity, insanity, and more insanity," Lace said, and then rolled her eyes. "Girl, you know that damn man is crazy."

"And that's not new, so what makes it any different now?" I asked.

"Because I have to live with his crazy ass. I'm talking 24/7, all up in my shit all day every day."

"Then why did you move in with him?" Mo asked.

"Girl, you've met Royal. If I wouldn't have agreed, his crazy ass probably would have burned my whole apartment complex down. I'm trying to keep him out of jail," Lace laughed at herself.

43

"Lace, really?" Mo asked.

"Hell yeah, you have no idea," she said, and rolled her eyes.

"What about you, Laney?" I said, calling her by the nickname that Kay had for her.

"What about me?"

"You know I'm up at random times with Mani, so I know you haven't been coming home all week." All eyes were on Lane now.

"Yeah and?" she said.

"You moving out?" Lace asked with a grin.

"Nah, we're just chilling right now."

"Yeah, you're chillin alright. Kay is chillin all up in them guts," Lace said.

"You're special," Lane said, and threw a pillow at Lace.

"You're grown, boo. Do your thing. I'm just glad you finally saw the light. I thought Kay was going to kidnap and rape you for holding out on him."

"Lace!" I yelled, and then laughed.

"What? Don't act like you weren't all thinking the same thing. I'm just saying. Had that man walking around all pitiful."

"True," I said. Lane just looked at the three of us and laughed.

"I swear, y'all are doing the most," she glanced at Mo. "They're not usually this over the top."

"Yes we are, don't lie to Mo like that. She might as well get used to it," I said.

"Exactly, this is us, take it or leave it. We're a few screws short of completion, but we'll always have your back," Lace said.

Mo looked at us and smiled. "I can live with that. You guys keep me laughing. I was nervous about meeting you, because I knew you guys were already tight, but Karter was like they're cool, don't worry; but every time I asked him how you were, he was like you just have to be around them to see. Now I understand why. There's no way to explain you guys." Me, Lace, and Lane looked at each other and then laughed.

"Dang boo, are we that bad?" Lace said.

"No," Mo yelled through a laugh. "It's all good. I work so much that most of my friends are really just industry associates, so our relationships are more professional, but your guys are like the real deal. I guess you never know what you're missing until you actually get to experience it."

"Amen sister," I said.

"Well, you're stuck with us now so welcome to the crazy crew," Lane said.

"Yep, we'll get to the initiation part later, it involves some duct tape, feathers and, a lot of baby oil," Lace said. Mo looked at Lace confused.

"Girl, stop looking like that. I'm just playing."

"You're so damn stupid. Where the hell did that come from?" I asked.

"I just said the first thig that popped in my head."

"Uh boo, we really don't want to know what you and Royal are into, some stuff should just be kept private," Lane said, making all of us laugh

"Oh hell no. His bipolar ass is crazy, but not a damn closet freak. You can kill that," Lace said, trying not to laugh.

"I'm just saying, to each his own," Mo said.

"I know, right? I just had all kinds of unwanted visuals pop in my head. That's just nasty," I said

"Shut up Free, you should be grateful. I know you're all sexually frustrated since you just had Imani. Your ass still has four weeks to go," Lace said.

"True," Lane said. "How's that working out for you, Free?"

I frowned. "It's not, so let's just let that go for now."

"Ah boo. You need a little King in your life," Lace said with a grin.

"She needs a lot of King in a lot of places," Lane said.

"Oh my God, you guys need to stop," Mo said, and gave me a sympathetic look before she laughed.

"Forget you and you," I pointed to Lace, and then Lane.

"I'm just playing, boo. Hang in there. The drought will be over before you know it," Lace said.

I just shook my head and laughed. My girls were crazy, and I loved them to death. I swear, I couldn't see life without them. We spent the next few hours laughing and talking before we planned our next girl's day, and then everyone went home. After everyone was gone and it was just me and Mani, I settled in bed, armed with the remote and plenty of snacks. I was about to chill and then crash until my man got home.

I woke up when I felt Diego climb into bed, kiss me on the back of my neck, wrap his arms around my body.

"What time is it?"

"Late, go back to sleep," he whispered against my ear before he tugged on my earlobe.

47

"Damn, a nigga is not going to make it six weeks, Free. You sure we have to wait that long?" Diego asked as he kissed the back of my neck.

"You'll survive, but maybe I can help you with that."

I pulled away from Diego and forced him onto his back. I didn't care how faithful Diego had been lately, or how reformed he claimed to be, six weeks was a long time for a man that was used to having sex-and a lot of it. I refused to give my man a green light to run to the next bitch, so I was going to have to take matters into my own hands.

"What are you doing?" Diego asked when he felt my hands in his boxers, but I didn't answer. I figured actions speak louder than words, and he knew the second my tongue glided across his head.

I let my hands glide up and down his shaft as I took him in my mouth, and I just did what naturally felt right. I had no clue what I was doing, and other than a few tips from my girls I was basically winging, but Diego didn't seem to mind because after a few minutes, I felt his hands in my hair and he was mumbling something that I couldn't understand-until I heard my name.

"Shit Free."

I could feel his body tense up and he pulled away from me, covering the head of his dick with his hand as he came. He laid there for a minute before he climbed out of bed, walked into the bathroom, and damn near slammed the door, which woke up Imani. I climbed out of bed to get her, but he opened the bathroom door and walked over to her bassinet.

"I got her," he said, and leaned down to pick her up. I walked up behind him, kissed him on the back, and let my arms wrap around his waist. I didn't know why, but for some reason he seemed like something was bothering him.

King

When I felt Free kiss me on my back and then wrap her arms around me, I wanted to shove her ass away, but I had my baby girl in my arms. The closer Free was to me, the more pissed I got.

Free was a virgin when we first got together, and it had been almost a year, and not once had she ever given me head, and tonight out of the blue she did that shit–and not like any amateur I knew. I mean, she wasn't shutting shit down but fuck, she handled that shit good enough to make my ass cum after only a few minutes, so that had me pissed. Where the fuck did she learn that shit from, because I damn sure didn't teach her.

My baby girl was asleep again, so I pushed away from Free and laid Imani back in her bassinet. She was so damn beautiful; watching her tiny little face was the only thing keeping me from jacking Free up right now. I had never laid hands on her and I never thought that I would, but the way I was feeling right now, I wanted to wrap my hands around her neck.

I walked over and sat on the side of the bed, and Free tried to position herself between my legs but I pushed her away, trying to give myself a minute so that I could find out what the fuck was going on.

"What's wrong?" The moon was shining through the blinds, so I could see a light glow on her face just enough to see her eyes.

"Who the fuck taught you how to do that shit, because I damn sure didn't," I asked calmly, and I knew the question was fucked up, but I needed some answers.

"Nobody taught me anything," Free finally said after she looked at me like I had two heads. "I mean, aside from talking to my girls, I just did it."

"Don't fucking lie to me Free, have you been with someone else?"

The look on her face gave me the answer I was looking for, and I knew right then that I was dead ass wrong-but damn, I had to ask, and she went in on me for that shit.

"You are unfucking-beliveable. When the fuck am I supposed to have time to be with someone else, Dey? If I'm not with you, you have people driving me around or following me, and you know damn well I'm not going to bring anybody to our house, so when the fuck am I supposed to be with someone else? I swear, I fucking hate you sometimes. You're a certified asshole." Free tried to walk away from me, but I jumped up and grabbed her around the waist before I locked her in my arms.

"Calm down. I'm sorry ma. That shit was fucked up and I know it, but damn you had a brother on edge. You can't go from zero to a hundred with some shit like that and then not expect me to think you've been practicing. That was your first time hitting me off and I didn't have to tell you shit, so you had my mind wandering. Just the thought of you being with someone else had me ready to kill everything moving, so I said some fucked up shit and I'm sorry." Free didn't say a word, but I could feel her still trying to pull away from me.

"Don't be mad, I'm sorry." I started kissing her on her neck before I worked my way to her collarbone, and then her shoulder. I could feel her body relax a little, but I could tell she was still mad.

"You forgive me?" I asked.

"No, you're an asshole," she said, but I could tell she was letting it go.

"I'm your asshole though," I backed up and sat on the edge of the bed, pulling her with me.

"I'm not you, Dey. I wouldn't cheat," she said, trying to remind me that I was the one who had issues with commitment, and she was right. Free was loyal and all she wanted was me. Even though I knew that, it still crossed my mind that there was always a possibility that she could cheat, especially after everything that I had put her through.

"I know that, and you also know that's not me anymore. This right here is all I need, so you don't have to worry about that. It's just us. I promise."

Free didn't say anything, so I let it go. I knew she still had doubt, so I wasn't going to press the issue, but I meant that shit. I wasn't about to lose Free for some shit that was temporary. I knew what I wanted, and she was right here in my arms.

"Come on." I climbed back in bed, and Free reluctantly joined me. When I had her securely in my arms, I kissed her on the top of her head.

"You know I love you, right?" Free's stubborn ass ignored me.

"Free, I know you hear me."

"I hear you, but I'm still mad."

"You can be mad all you want, but you better answer me," I said playfully. She still didn't say anything.

"You know I love you, right?'

"I know Dey, now shut up before you wake Mani up again."

"Tell you love me." I bit down on her shoulder, causing her to punch me.

"I love you, now go to sleep." I tightened my grip on her and closed my eyes, and within minutes I felt myself drifting.

The next morning, I woke up early, still tired as hell since I'd literally went to sleep only hours ago. We had been working hard as hell trying to get shit worked out after combining our operations. Karter and Kay had a nice little set up, but with Los fucking with them we had to be extra careful.

I called Royal, knowing his ass wasn't going to be up, but we needed to start making plans for our next shipment. Even though we damn near tripled our last shipment from Del, we were still running low since we covered what Karter and Kay lost when Los hit their spot, and shit was selling like crazy.

Royal and I decided to meet with Del to see what the fuck was up with him, because we needed to either find a new connect or re-up with Del in order to keep our shit moving on the streets.

"Wake yo ass up!" I yelled into the phone the second Royal answered. It was just after 7:00, and I knew he was nowhere near awake.

"King, you're really gonna make me shoot your dumb ass. Why the fuck you yelling in my ear, bruh? That shit isn't cool."

I just laughed. "Get up. We're scheduled to meet Del at 10:00."

"That's in three hours, chill the fuck out. I got this."

"You don't have shit. You're late for everything, so get up."

"I'm hanging up now and if you call me back, I'm clocking your ass as soon as I see you."

"Man fuck you and get yo ass out of bed. I'm about to call Shine and then I'm calling you back in an hour to make sure your up." I hung up on him and called Shine.

"What's good bruh, we meet Del at 10:00, you ready?"

"Yeah I'm good on that." Shine's ass sounded either high or drunk; I couldn't tell which one.

"The fuck wrong with you? It's too early to be on one."

"I fucked up, King."

"Awe hell, what now?"

"Meka left my ass. I really fucked up this time."

"The fuck you do, Stanly?" I asked, calling him by his government name.

"Long story bruh. I'll tell you when I see you."

"Damn, it must be some serious shit. You need me to swing by and get you? Your ass sounds blitzed."

"Nah I'm straight, just tired a fuck. I've been up all night, but let me go so I can get my ass in the shower."

"Aight bruh. I'm out."

I ended the call, wondering what the hell he did to make Meka leave him. Hell, she probably caught his ass cheating again, but I wasn't too stressed. She was damn near five months pregnant and she loved his ass. She might spaz out on him for a minute, but she wasn't going anywhere. Or at least I hoped not.

I walked back upstairs to check on Free and Imani, and sure enough Imani's little ass was up, grinning and shit. This little girl was my pride and joy. She was such a good baby; she hardly ever cried, and she was damn near sleeping through the night at only two weeks old. That shit had me and Free both freaked out, because we would have to wake her up to feed her. I picked her up and held her in my arm while she looked up at me. Imani had me wrapped around her tiny little fingers already. That shit was insane, but I was loving it.

"Look at mommy. She's over there knocked out," I said as I glanced at Free, and then focused on Imani again.

"That's cool though, because you'd rather be with daddy right now any way, right?"

I kissed Imani on both of her chubby cheeks. She was so beautiful, a perfect blend of me and Free, but she had my dark curly hair, which made her look like my twin. As I walked around our bedroom with my baby girl in my arms, my phone rang; I stepped out the room, closed the door, and decided to head to my office.

"Yeah," I said as soon as I hit the first step.

"Good morning, King. I didn't wake you, did I?" Hearing Delgado's voice had me wanting to cock my gun. I hated snakes, and right now that's how I felt about him. After Solo found the footage of Sandra leaving his place, it had all of us feeling like he was on some bullshit so after today, if he didn't have a grand fucking explanation for that shit then we were finding a new connect.

"Nah, what's up?"

"Are we still on for our meeting this morning?"

"Yeah we're good."

"Wonderful, just checking. We have a lot to discuss."

"You're damn straight we do."

Del chuckled like his ass didn't have a care in the world, which pissed me off. I didn't care how much man power he had, I would shoot his ass my damn self and not flinch if I didn't like what the fuck he had to say.

"I'll see you at 10:00, King. I look forward to it."

"Yeah."

I ended the call and went back upstairs, straight to Mani's room to change her. I looked around and shook my head. It looked like the damn room threw up pink and silver. Free went overboard with this shit, but it was definitely fit for my little princess. After I had Mani changed, I picked her up and held her against my shoulder so that I could head back downstairs, but Free came walking in with a bottle in her hand.

"How long she been up?" Free asked, reaching for her. Normally I wouldn't have handed her off so easily, but I needed to get dressed so I didn't fight her on it.

"Not long." When Free had Imani securely in her arms, I kissed Free on the neck and tried to hug her, but she stepped away from me.

"You still mad about that shit? Damn Free, I said I was sorry."

Her stubborn ass just rolled her eyes and walked out the room, and I would have said something to her but my phone started ringing, so I left it alone for now.

"Yo, what up Karter?"

"Shit tired as fuck," Karter said.

"That's because your ass don't sleep for shit, bruh."

He laughed, "You right, but what time are you meeting with Del?"

"10:00, what's up?"

"Shit is too quiet right now. I can't get eyes on Los, and it's giving me a bad feeling."

"Yeah, I was thinking that shit too."

"I've got Sasha right now, but I'm taking her to my mom in a little while. I think we need to meet up and try and figure some shit out."

"Aight bet. I'll hit you up after we finish up with Del. Where's Kay?"

"Shit I don't know. I haven't talked to him since last night. I'm about to hit him up right now, so I'll let him know."

"Aight bet."

I ended the call and then went back into our room, where I found Free feeding Imani. The second I walked in the room she rolled her eyes at me, but the two of them sitting there made me smile so I let that shit go and walked into the closet.

"You leaving?" I didn't answer Free until I walked out of the closet.

"Oh, so you're talking to me now?" I asked with a smirk.

"I shouldn't be," she said, so I walked over and kissed her on the cheek.

"Yeah, I have a meeting with Shine and Royal, and then I think we're meeting up with Karter and Kay. Why what's up?"

"Nothing. Just asking."

"What are you getting into today?"

"Meka's coming over since she couldn't make it last night," Free said.

"Oh yeah?" was all I said, trying to see if she knew what was going down between Meka and Shine.

"Yeah, she was upset about something and said she needed to talk." Damn, Shine must have really fucked up if Meka was calling in reinforcement.

"Aight, well I'm about to shower and get dressed so I can head out."

I walked in the bathroom and shut the door. I had to get my mind right; I was just hoping whatever the fuck was going on with Shine and Meka didn't affect his ability to handle business. Now was the time for any of us to be off our game. We were right in the middle of a street war, and possibly about to have to switch shit up with our product. I needed everybody on point and focused, so Shine was going to have to press pause on the personal shit for now.

Shine

I looked down at my phone again, and it was Asia just like it thought.

"Fuck," I mumbled.

This shit was beyond messed up. I hadn't seen or heard from her ass in eight months, and then she showed up at my damn house telling Meka that she was pregnant. Meka was five months, carry my son, and now Asia claimed to be eight months, carrying my daughter.

I couldn't really say, shit because it was damn sure likely that Asia was telling the truth. We had been chilling hard and I knew I was wrong, but I did hit raw on the regular so I was almost positive that her baby could be mine. I got careless and did some dumb shit, and now I possibly had two babies on the way.

To say that Meka was pissed did the situation no justice. She tried to stab my ass before she packed her shit and headed straight to her mother's house. That was the last place I needed her to be. Wanda kept up too much shit and she hated my ass. She loved my money, but believe me when I say she couldn't stand me. Meka had a bad habit of telling her mom our business, and I hated that shit. I kept trying to tell Meka that we could argue and fight and be over that shit, but her mom wouldn't let it go so she threw it in my face every chance she got. In fact, the only time she wasn't talking shit about me was when I was handing off a stack, but that was Meka's mom so I let that it go.

Trust me when I say now that Asia was potentially carrying my child, Wanda was at her house going in on me. She was probably filling out child support papers, while trying to convince Meka to leave me at this very moment. Wanda loved her daughter, but she loved money even more and she knew that Meka carrying my baby was a guaranteed check, so if she could get my money without having to deal with me, I knew that was smiling from ear to ear.

My phone went off again and I knew that Asia was going to keep blowing me up, so I just answered.

"What?"

"You don't have to be so rude, Shine. I'm sorry if our little situation is fucking with your happy home, but this baby is real so your little princess is just gonna have to get over it."

"Asia, what the fuck do you want?"

"I want to see if you will meet me so we can talk."

That shit was funny as hell. "Talk about what? We don't have shit to talk about until you have that damn baby and we get the results back. If it's mine, then we'll talk."

"It's yours, trust me. You know it and I know it."

"Yeah we'll see, but trust if it is, the only thing we'll be talking about is my child. I still don't want shit to do with you."

"You sure about that?"

"One hundred percent."

"Yeah, well time will tell. I'm due any day now, so get ready," she said, and then hung up.

I grabbed my keys and left my house. Once I was in my car, I tried Meka once more and she sent my call straight to voicemail. She had been ignoring me all night, but she was gonna talk to me one way or another. She knew I hated her mom and figured that she could hide out there, but as soon as we were done handling business I was going to get her; even if I had to walk in there guns blazing, she was going home with me. Fuck the bullshit. I messed up and I know I did, but she wasn't leaving my ass.

I laughed as I started my car, because the first thing that came to mind was King telling Free that the only way she was leaving him was in a body bag. I thought King was crazy as hell for saying that shit, but now I felt the same way. Love will have you saying and doing some shit that you never saw yourself doing but trust me, Meka wasn't going no damn where.

"What the fuck did you do?" Royal asked the second I got out my car. He was standing outside the warehouse smoking a blunt.

"I got caught slipping in a major way." I walked up to him and leaned against the wall.

"You know Meka called all the girls and their having a *we hate Shine* meeting at King's spot. Your ass must have done something major," Royal said with a smirk.

We both looked up at the same time when King came pulling up on his bike. It was too damn cold to be on a damn bike, but his crazy ass didn't give a fuck. January in NC was no joke. He pulled his helmet off, locking crazy as fuck with all that wild ass hair.

"Yo, you know your girl is on her way to my house and she's out for blood. She called in back up and they're probably plotting right now on how to take your ass out. What the fuck did you do?" King said the second he was close to us.

I just shook my head and walked in the warehouse, followed by the two of them. It was 9:30, so we had a minute before Del was supposed to show up. Once we were in the office, I fell back into the sofa while King and Royal stood in front of me waiting.

"Well muthafucker, start talking," King said, looking impatient as fuck.

"You remember Asia?" I eyed both of them, waiting.

That bad ass chick from Charlotte?"

"Yeah, well she showed up at my house last night and she's pregnant. Like *about to drop that load any day* pregnant."

"Damn Shine, that's fucked up. That's some deep shit right there. Is it yours?"

"Strong possibility."

"Meka is gonna kill your ass bruh," King said.

"Shit, she already tried. She almost stabbed me last night."

"Oh shit word? And now she's about to have the crew all up in her head. Yeah, you're fucked bruh."

"Shit I know, but I don't give a fuck. Whether that baby is mine or not, me and Meka are gonna have to figure this shit out. She's not going anywhere. That's dead."

"I don't know bruh. That some serious shit to deal with, and you know Wanda hates your ass. You know she's been all in her head telling her to leave your ass," Royal said.

"Man fuck her mom. She's just mad because I won't fuck her. I be wanting to tell Meka that shit but I know she won't believe me, but the way her mom is always coming at me isn't right. She got some shit with her." King and Royal both looked at me and busted out laughing.

65

"I knew that shit. I told King a long time ago that you were hitting her mom off like you fucking her too."

"Man hell no, I wouldn't do no shit like that. I mean, she could get it but I wouldn't do that shit to Meka.

Shit, Meka's mom looked good as fuck. She kept her shit tight, which was one of the main reasons why I rocked with Meka so hard. I knew exactly what she was going to look like when she got older, and a brother couldn't take any chances. Age wasn't always kind to women, and I knew that was messed up, but I needed to be sure that Meka was going to be straight.

"See, that's your problem right there. You're thinking with the wrong head," King said.

"King, shut the hell up. I know you're not talking. Free caught your ass with your dick in somebody's mouth!" I yelled.

Royal laughed and then looked at King. "He's got a point, bruh."

"Man, both of you can kiss my ass. I might have got caught slipping, but you best believe she was the only one carrying my baby, and that shit right there is not gonna change."

"Damn King. You're cold for that," Royal said with a grin.

"Man fuck. I have to figure this shit out cause I promise you, Meka's ass is not about to be up in another nigga's face with my kid. That shit isn't happening. Somebody will die first."

"Yo, calm you cheating ass down. We'll figure this shit out, but you know you're about to have to undo all the shit that Free and them are about to put in her head. They go hard," King said just as the alarm went off, letting us know Del hit the driveway.

"Now let's just hope this muthafucker doesn't come up in here talking some fuck shit," King said as the three of us made our way to the door.

"Shit let him, the way I'm feeling right now I need to shoot somebody to get my head right," I said.

"Yo Royal, take that fool's gun before he fucks around and shoots Del's ass for real. We don't have time for that shit right now." Royal just laughed but I was serious as fuck.

"King, Royal, Shine. Thank you for meeting with me," Delgado said as she stood in front of us smiling. He had two men with him, one on each side, but that shit was normal since he never traveled alone.

"We need you to clear up a few things," King said, and handed Del the envelope that had the prints of Sandra leaving his place. Solo printed stills from the video he found and gave them to us.

Del opened the envelope and scanned the photos before he handed them to the body guard.

"I figured this was going to be a problem, so I came prepared as well," Del said as he nodded towards the same body guard who pulled out a small recorder.

"This should clear that up," Del said, and then pressed play; a conversation he had with Sandra began to play.

"If that was the case, then you would have already done that Sandra and besides, I have no beef with King, Royal, and Shine. They have always been honest, upfront, and they buy more than anyone else I'm dealing with, so unfortunately you're on your own."

When it was done, Delgado looked at the three of us.

"As you can see, the only loyalty I have is to money, so it was not my place to get involved in that situation. I made that very clear to Sandra, so we have no issues as far as I'm concerned.

"I see you didn't feel like we deserved a head's up either, and that shit was shady as fuck Del," Royal said.

"As I said before, it was not my place to get involved. I was not going to help or hurt Sandra's situation, but if you feel like I did you an injustice I understand. I would hate to lose your business, but that is your decision to make. I simply wanted you to be very clear about where my loyalties lie and as I stated, money is my only concern."

"Let us discuss it and we'll get back to you," King said.

We all shook Delgado's hand, and he did that damn hugging shit. He was too caught up in that mafia life for me. Del left, and the three of us went back to the office.

"So what now?" I asked. Royal was on the sofa next to me, while King was leaning back on the edge of the desk.

"Man, I don't trust that shit," Royal said, which I expected. His perspective was different from mine and King's since it was his mother that was trying to fuck us over.

"Yo, I don't trust that shit either, but we're still standing and Del could have set us up on some real shit. He might not have given us a heads up, but we know for sure he stayed out of it," I said.

"True and think about it. He's not willing to fuck us over on that type of level. We buy a lot of shit from him, and now that Kay and Karter are on, we'll be buying a lot more, so I say we roll with it for now," King said, eyeing Royal.

He looked at me and then King and could tell he was processing.

"Look you know it's all or nothing so if you're not feeling this shit then we'll look into some other options but we've got a lot going on right now and I think it's best if we stay with Del at least for now," I said,'

"Fuck it. I'm in. I just hope this shit works out, because I promise you, on everything–I'll kill Del's bitch ass myself if it turns out he's on some fuck shit," Royal said, and he was serious as hell.

*****

"Your ass must have had hit last night?" Royal asked Karter, who was currently stretched out on the sofa with his arms folded across his face. He would respond if one of us addressed him directly, but for the most part he was just listening.

"Nah why?" he said without moving his arms. His eyes were still closed.

"Shit, your ass is over there in zombie mode," I said.

He chuckled a little. "Nah, just on the grind. I need to find Los before he finds me."

"So how did that shit go with Del?" Kay asked.

"We're good on that, so we need to figure out what we need and the next buy we make, you and Karter need to be there."

"So you haven't seen or heard anything from Los?" I asked Karter.

"Nah, he was blowing up Mo's phone so I broke that shit and got her a new one. He doesn't know how to find her so shits been quiet, but he thinks like I think. Right now he's just watching and waiting. He's moving in the shadows trying to figure out my moves so he will know his move. It's a process, and the bad thing is I'll never see that shit coming."

"What's the move then?" Royal asked.

"We just have to shake shit up. His people are not going to be as careful as he is, so we can draw him out by fucking with them. The down side to that is we don't know shit about him or how he operates, so we'll always be moving blind because we don't have enough time to figure that shit out."

Karter still had his eyes closed. and his voice was calm and controlled. You could tell he was a killer. He had the type of personality that was hard to read. You never knew what you were getting; one minute he was flying off the hand; while the next he was calm as fuck; like he had ice in his veins.

"Well let's do what the fuck we gotta do then, 'cause this sitting and waiting shit is not my thing. I need to know Free, Mira, and my baby girl are safe," King said.

"Aight. I'm on it. Let me get with Solo. I need him to check on a few things for me, and then we'll make some moves. I'll hit everybody up later." Karter was finally sitting upright, but he had no expression as he looked around at all of us.

"I guess I'll take my ass home and try figure out what to do about Meka."

"What's going on with Meka? She good, bruh?" Kay asked.

"Hell no she's not good. Mr. Straight shooter over here just found out he's got another one on the way, and Meka is currently at my house with the crew plotting about how to kill his ass."

"Damn Shine, it's like that?" Kay said. My hand went across my forehead, and then through my hair before I leaned back and began twisting a piece of it.

"That shit is not my fault. Who the fuck gets pregnant, leaves for eight months, and then shows up a few days before it's time to drop that load, talking about it's time?"

"That's some fuck shit," I said, and it was. Hell, if I had known I would have had time to prepare and wrap my brain around that shit.

"The fuck you mean it's not your fault bruh," Karter looked at me like I was crazy. "You went up in that shit raw. You've been with Meka for four years, right? That means your ass got caught slipping," he said with a smirk.

"Hell yeah he did, and I'm about to go pick Laney's insecure ass up right now. I don't need her getting any kind of ideas in her head. You know if one of us fucks up, we all fuck up," Kay said. I just laughed, because he was right. Their asses stuck together on everything.

"Damn, I didn't even think about that shit," Royal said. "Lace stays on the fence with me. I'm 'bout to call her right now and tell her to take her ass home."

"Kill that shit. They've been together for the past four hours, the damage is done."

"I'm telling you now Shine, if I don't get any pussy tonight because of this shit, I'm fucking your ass up," Kay said.

"Get in line muthafucker, because I can guarantee Meka has already got some shit waiting on him. Trust that," Royal said, making all of us laugh. Hell, I laughed too cause I knew that shit was true. I guess it was time to get this shit over with. The longer I waited, the more time she had to think about it.

Meka

I had been at my mom's house for less than a day, and she was literally driving me crazy. The second I walked in from chilling with my girls, she was all over me trying to find out what the deal was, had I talked to him, what he said, and was the baby really his. I mean damn, she was more invested in this than I was.

My phone went off again, and I didn't even bother checking the screen before I sent it to voicemail, because I knew it was Shine. My girls were torn about the situation. Mo and Free were on team Shine, while Lace and Lane were like leave him. I just didn't know what to do. I had been with Stanley for four years, and I knew he cheated, but at least he always kept it from me. Never once had I been confronted by any of his hoes. I had caught a few side eyes and hard stares from women I had a feeling he was creeping with, but for the most part, they stayed in their lane; but this situation was something that I couldn't leave at just an assumption. She was most definitely pregnant, and all Shine could say was *it's possible*.

What the fuck is that? It could be possible, and when I asked his crazy ass if he had unprotected sex with her, his hand went across his head and then he began massaging his temple. I just walked away and started packing my shit. He stood there arguing with me the entire time, telling me that I wasn't going anywhere-until I calmly walked in the kitchen, picked up the biggest knife that I could get my hands on, got ready to aim it at him. He didn't take me serious until it actually pierced his skin. I was tempted to grab one of his guns, but I was so mad that I probably would have pulled the trigger, and I didn't want him dead; I just wanted him to hurt the way I was hurting.

"I can't believe he did this to us. I mean really, after four years and that's what we get?" My mother stood in front of the television like her father was a fucking glass maker staring at me; and why the fuck did she keep saying we? Was she fucking Shine too?

"What's this we shit, ma? I mean damn. You act like this is more about you than me," I rolled my eyes and then lifted myself off the sofa. I didn't want to go home, but I didn't want to be here around her either.

"Watch your mouth, Tameka. You will not disrespect me in my house."

"Your house," I laughed and walked away.

"Yes my house." She followed behind me. I swear I loved my mother, but she couldn't leave well enough alone.

"Ma, I'm tired. I think I'm going to bed." I wasn't in the mood to argue with her.

"No, you're grown and I know you were about to say some slick shit about this being my house, so speak you mind little girl."

"Night ma. I'm going to bed." I turned to walk down the hall towards my old room, but she kept going.

"Yeah that's what I thought."

"See, that shit right there is why I hate being around you. I love you ma I swear, but you need to stay in your land. This house might be in your name, but Shine paid for it. That car out there in the driveway that you forever bragging about? He paid for that shit too. But the crazy thing is that you're always giving him your ass to kiss. It's partly my fault because I tell you more than I should, and he tolerates it because he loves me but honestly, you need to respect him more; appreciate the things he does for you and stay the fuck out of our business. I apologize for being disrespectful, but it seems like that's the only way you hear me sometimes."

My mother looked at me shocked, like she couldn't believe what I just said, but she snapped out of it quickly.

"Oh so I see how we're doing it now. He's got some other bitch pregnant, while you're pregnant I might add, and all you can think to do is stand here and cuss your mother."

"Night ma, I'm going to bed."

I didn't have the energy to deal with here, and I wasn't going to try. I walked down the hall and with my back to my mother, she continued mumbling.

"Ungrateful ass. Cussing me because your man doesn't know how to keep his dick in his pants. I told her that shit was going to happen dealing with a street nigga."

I just laughed as I entered my room. She didn't have a problem with Shine being a street nigga when he was dropping stacks in her bank account.

I laid down on my bed, staring at the ceiling and rubbing my stomach as my baby boy began moving around. I was so in love with my son, but being in love with him reminded me of how much I hated his father, so I was stuck in the middle of a bad situation. My phone started vibrating again and I was about to shut it off for good, but I realized it was Free and decided to answer.

"Hey boo, you feeling any better?" she asked.

"Not really, but oh well. I guess it is what it is," I said, and then let out a long sigh.

"Have you talked to him?"

"Nope, and I'm not going to. I can't deal with him right now," I said.

"Dey just got home and he said that Shine was on his way out there."

"I hope not, because it will be a wasted trip."

"The situation is totally messed up and he was wrong-hell, he was beyond wrong-but are you really ready to walk away?"

"I don't know what I'm ready for, but that one mistake just cost him eighteen years, Free. It's not like you catching King with Lauren. She's having his baby, Free. I don't know if I can deal with that. You know how that shit goes; bitches refuse to let go, and I'm not dealing with that shit. Always wondering if it's about the kid or if they're still fucking."

"I know boo, it's complicated, but he loves you. You know that and you already said that he told you that he didn't want anything to do with her even, if the baby was his, so you can make it work if that's what you want. You have to think about your baby and your situation. Do you really want to do that by yourself?"

"Hell no, but I can and I will if that's want it comes to."

"But is that what you want?"

"I'm not going to stay with him just because of this baby, Free."

"That's not what I'm saying, Meka. I'm saying he messed up. Nah, he royally fucked up on some major type shit, but he loves you and I can guarantee that his will be enough for him to get his shit together. I know him Meka, he doesn't want to be without you, so just think about that because you don't want to be without him either. I'm not saying be one of those women who let their men say and do anything, but I am saying that some situations are worth saving, and yours is worth saving."

"That's easy for you to say; King got his shit together and is doing the right thing, but he also didn't fuck up and get someone else pregnant. Would you have stayed if he did?'

"I don't know boo, but Dey and I are still new; we haven't even hit the year mark so we don't have the history like you do, so it's different. I let Dey get away with a lot more than I should have, and I promise you that if he decides to take that route again, then it's not likely that I'll stay. You two have a whole lot more invested than we did, so jut think about it Meka and if you decide it's not what you want, then let me be the first call you make and I'll help you get rid of the body- no questions asked."

I couldn't help but laugh. She was so damn stupid, but I loved my girl.

"You're crazy Free, but I appreciate that. No body, no case. Isn't that what the guys say?"

"Yeah, but I promise, they never thought it could possibly apply to them," Free said

"I'll call you tomorrow. I think I'm going to bed."

"Aight, love you boo."

"I love you too girl."

79

*****

"Meka, we need to talk."

I opened my eyes and stared right into Shine's face. He was sitting in a chair next to my bed looking like he had been up for days, but his ass still looked sexy as hell.

"What are you doing her, Stanly?" He knew that I never called him by his real name unless I was mad, so hearing it made his face tighten up.

"I'm here because we need to talk."

"Talk about what Stanley, she's pregnant; it might be yours, and I need to figure out what's next for me. There's nothing to talk about."

"The fuck you mean you have to figure out what's next for you? So it's just you now?"

I sat up in my bed and crossed my legs so that I was sitting Indian style, and of course his eyes went straight to my stomach.

"Yeah, it's just me right now. You made that decision for me when you decided to go lay up in the next bitch making love connections and babies."

"Don't say that shit, Meka. You're the only person I love and I put that on everything. I messed up and I know it, but I don't love that bitch so don't get it twisted."

I just rolled my eyes. "Yeah, well it doesn't really matter because your daughter will be here any day now. You need to start figuring out how you're going to handle that."

"No, we need to figure that shit out. I know it's a fucked up situation, but if that's my kid then *WE* need to figure this shit out. I'm never going to turn my back on my kid Meka, you know I can't do that shit. I will not be like my father but trust me, my kid will be the only responsibility I have when it comes to that situation. I don't want shit to do with Asia, and a baby is not going to change that. This is what I want and all that I want."

He looked at me with those damn sad eyes and I just wanted to kiss his sexy lips, but my heart was telling me to stay away.

"I don't want this, Stanley. It's just too much and I don't want it," I said as I felt the tears building.

He looked at me with murder in his eyes. He was angry, but I didn't care. I didn't have a say in him getting somebody else pregnant, but I did have a say in whether or not I was going to stay around to deal with it.

"The fuck you mean you don't want this? You don't want my son, you don't want me? Is that what you mean Tameka, because neither of those is an option. I know I did some fuck shit, but you don't get to just walk away like I don't mean shit to you, like these past four years don't mean shit to you."

"Why not? It obviously didn't mean shit to you. We are currently having a conversation about you having a baby with the next bitch, so apparently I didn't rate high on your importance scale, and yes I want my son. He's about the only thing that I know I want right now. I just hate that he's a part of you. What I don't want is this bullshit relationship that I've been holding on to for the past four years."

Shine just sat there looking at me like he was trying to decide what he wanted to say, and honestly I didn't know if he could say anything that would change how I felt. True enough I loved him, but I just didn't see how I could be around him and watch him love another child. A child that wasn't ours. He cheated and as crazy as it sounded, I could actually get over that part, but that baby was going to be a constant reminder. Having that baby in our home and around me would always make me remember that I wasn't enough.

I knew that Shine would never turn his back on a child of his, because he knew what that felt like. His mother struggled to raise him on her own when his father walked out and never looked back, and then his sister's father did the exact same thing. He stepped up and became everything that Reesey needed because he never wanted her to feel what he felt by not having a father in her life, so I knew that if that baby was his then he was going to love that baby with everything that he was, and I didn't know if I could stay around to watch that.

Yeah, it might have been a selfish way of thinking because that baby is the innocent one in all this, but I couldn't help it. I deserved to have whatever feelings about it I wanted to, so I didn't feel bad about that at all. I hated that baby, and I hated him for creating it.

Stanley stood up, but kept his eyes on me the entire time. He pulled his sweatshirt over his head and then his t-shirt before he sat down next to me on the bed. He grabbed my hand and placed it on his chest, covering the infinity tattoo with our names in it.

"This is not bullshit, Meka. I may have done some foul shit, but this is not bullshit and you know it. You're mad and you're hurt, but you love me and you know that I love you."

He kept his eyes on me as he lifted that same hand and kissed the matching tattoo that I had on the inside of my wrist before he let it go. I watched as he pulled his t-shirt over his head again, covering his perfectly carved chest, after which he followed with his hoodie and then just stood there watching me.

"I'll give you a minute if that's what you need, but you're coming home and we're going to figure this out." Shine leaned down and wiped the stream of tears from my check before he kissed me, and then moved towards the door.

"You're coming home Meka, and I mean that shit." Something in his voice let me know that he wasn't playing, but it didn't matter because it wasn't his choice to make.

After he was gone, I just laid down in my bed, closed my eyes, and cried. I was so angry with him, but I was more hurt. I had always been there for him. I was the perfect girlfriend. I loved him through all his bullshit and never once cheated. I didn't need to, because I loved Shine and he was all I wanted. He wasn't perfect, yet he loved me and made it so that I didn't want for anything, but all the money in the world couldn't erase the fact that he was about to have a child with another woman.

Having his child growing inside of me created a connection to him that I just couldn't explain, and now someone else had that same connection. How could he not feel something for her since she was carrying his baby? She was carrying his daughter, and I had seen the way that King immediately fell in love with Imani, so I knew that it would be the same for Shine. I didn't know if I could handle that, but could I really walk away?

I laid there in the dark with my hands on my stomach. My mind was all over the place, searching for answers that weren't going to come, so I just let go and let my mind drift. Maybe things would be better in the morning.

Karter

I had been sitting in my car for about three hours, just watching Los's spot. He was nowhere to be found, but his men were in and out all day. They had apparently just received a shipment of guns, because I noticed them moving a truck load of crates into their warehouse. Just like I suspected, his men were sloppy. They were careless and not really paying attention to their surroundings. I had been in the same spot for days watching them, and neither of them noticed. That's why I liked to keep my circle small. The more people you dealt with, the more you opened yourself up to make mistakes.

It had always been just me and Kay, so rocking with King, Shine, and Royal was taking me some time to get used to. I was used to making moves based of instinct, and now I had to involve not only Kay, but three others and it changed the way I handled business-well, company business that is. My hits were still private, and nobody had a say in any of that.

I decided to call it a day since it seemed like nothing with this situation had really changed, and there were still no sign of Los. I was tired as hell and hadn't really slept in days. Mo was on me because I hadn't really been home either, and I knew she missed me but I couldn't rest until I knew that she was going to be safe, so Los and his team were my priority right now.

After I started my car and pulled off, I decided to call Mo and check on her. It was late, but she usually tried to stay up to wait for me when she could.

"Hey baby, I'm heading that way, you good?"

"I'm fine, just hurry up. I miss you."

I just chuckled. "I'll be there soon. Be naked."

I ended the call and began speeding through traffic. I needed an escape, and right now all I could think about was being in between Mo's legs. That shit had me doing damn near 100 just so that I could get there.

After I parked and made my way through the lobby towards my elevator, I made sure to pay attention to my surroundings, mostly out of habit but especially now since I couldn't get eyes on Los. The last thing I needed was for him to catch me slipping. When I finally made it to my apartment and stepped inside, my phone rang so I pulled it out of my pocket and answered, realizing it was Kay.

"What up baby bruh, you good?"

"Yeah, I'm chilling, just checking in," Kay said.

I walked into my bedroom and found Mo, naked just like I asked with her knees in the air and legs wide open, giving me a full view of all her sweetness. I walked over to the bed and, still holding my phone in place with my shoulder, I slid two fingers inside of her. She lifted her head and kept her eyes on me as I stroked her insides.

"I just got home, so I'll hit you up later. I want to run something by you."

"Aight, that works."

I still had my eyes on Mo and could tell that her orgasm was building, which was sexy as hell because she bit down on her bottom lip and closed her eyes as she let her head fall back, extending her neck.

"Aight Kay. I'm out. Don't take your ass to sleep."

"Don't be all night muthafucker. Just cause your ass doesn't sleep doesn't mean that I don't sleep."

I laughed when Kay hung up on me. I tossed my phone on the bed before I crawled between Mo's legs. The second my tongue touched her clit, I felt her body start to pulse and she collapsed on the bed.

"I guess you did miss me," I said arrogantly.

"Shut up and take your clothes off," she said, sounding like she was out of breath.

I pulled my shirt off and tossed it on the floor before I stepped out of my Timbs, and then my jeans. Mo just watched as I climbed in-between her legs and kissed her.   Her hands went down my back before she reached down and tried to push me inside her.

"Chill Mo, let me do this," I said with a grin. I knew she wanted me, but I was purposely making her wait and she hated that shit.

I pulled back and began kissing her body. I let my tongue circle her nipple before I took it in my mouth and began gently sucking and tugging. Next, I trailed kisses down her chest until I reached her stomach. I smiled, thinking about my baby growing in there.

"Turn over." I grabbed Mo around the waist and helped her position herself on her stomach before I pressed my body against hers, with my head at her opening.

"Karter, stop playing," she moaned as I kissed the side of her face, and then the back of her neck

"You want me inside?" I whispered against her ear. Mo just nodded.

"Tell me what you want, Mo."

"I want you. I want to feel you inside me, Karter." Her voice was sexy and labored, and I couldn't take that shit anymore so I began slowly entering her. Inch by inch, I made my way inside until her body tensed up, and I began giving her what she wanted-long , deep strokes hitting everything within reach.

"Is this what you wanted, Mo?"

She didn't say a word; she just reached down and dug her nails into my thigh as I moved inside her. I slid my hand around her neck and gently squeezed as I went deeper inside her body, and as I picked up my pace, I could feel my nut building so I pulled out and turned her over. I wasn't ready for that shit yet.

Mo looked at me with those sexy ass eyes, and I dove in again. This time, her legs were across my arms and I could tell from the look on her face that it was too much for her. She bit down on her lip and closed her eyes as she held on to my arms so tight that I knew that she was drawing blood the way her nails pierced my skin. It didn't take long for both of us to reach the edge, and we came together. I released so hard that it took me a minute to recover before I could move again.

"My mother wants us to come visit," Mo said randomly as she laid her head on my chest, and I let my hand slid down her back.

"You know I can't do that shit right now, Mo," I glanced at her, but she wasn't looking at me so I let my hand go through her hair.

"I know. I was just telling you," She wanted us to go. I could hear it in her voice.

"You should go, though. I know you miss your father." Mo tolerated her mother, but she loved her father and I knew it was killing her to be away from him for so long.

She didn't say anything and I knew why. She didn't want to go alone and as much as she wanted to see her family, she didn't want to leave me.

"I don't want to go without you, and I'm tired of you sending me away." I clenched my fist and I could feel my pulse quicken, but with a few deep breaths I was able control it.

"I'm not sending you away, Mo. You and this baby are my priority, so I will do whatever the fuck I need to in order to keep you both safe," I said calmly.

"I know," was all she said.

I laid there with Mo for another hour until she went to sleep, and then I carefully slid my body away from hers, grabbed my phone and then walked into the living room, shutting the door behind me.

"Yo, you sleep," I asked as soon as Kay answered.

"Nah, I'm good what's up?"

"I've been watching their warehouse and I've pretty much got their routine down, so I was thinking that if we hit their shit then Los will definitely show his face.

"You think that's a good idea? If we hit their spot then it's putting a target on your back. He already wants you, so if you take his shit then he will be out for blood." I could hear the doubt in my brother voice.

"I'm not a bitch Kay, and I'm tired of sitting around. There's already a target on my back, so that shit's not gonna change. I just need this shit over with."

"Fuck, I do to but I don't want to lose you in the process. What if that shit goes wrong?"

"Come on Kay, you know I'm on my shit. I'm not about to let that muthafucker take me out."

"There's some shit you just can't control Karter, no matter how hard you try. I know you're good at what you do, but that's no guarantee that shit is gonna work out."

"Look. I'm not gonna hide from anybody. You know me well enough to know that, and I feel like that's what I'm doing by not going after him. This shit is about to end one way or another. We're meeting with King, Shine, and Royal tomorrow, and they're either in or not, but I'm hitting his spot tomorrow night and then when that muthafucker comes for me, I'm putting a bullet right in between his eyes."

"Aight, calm the fuck down. If you feel like this is what we need to do, then let's do that shit. Now take your ass to bed and I'll talk to you in the morning."

I could tell my brother wasn't happy, but fuck it. I needed this shit to be over. I stood in front of the window, looking down at the city as my mind drifted. I didn't know how this shit was going to play out, but it was going to end.

*****

When I woke up the next morning, Mo wasn't in bed so after I sat up and stretched, I climbed out of bed. I checked my phone, and it was after 10:00. This was the first time in a long time that I slept in. I guess my body finally shut down and took what it needed.

I went straight to the bathroom and when I was finished in there, I went to find Mo, figuring that she was in the living watching TV or doing yoga. She loved that shit while the only thing I loved about it was watching her do it.

After I searched my entire apartment and didn't find her, I immediately called her and when she didn't answer, I started getting dressed. She knew to always answer my calls no matter what was going on. I called downstairs and Davis, our daytime desk clerk, answered.

"Good morning Mr. Davidson what can I do for you?" Davis asked cheerfully.

"Did you see Mo leave this morning?"

"Yes sir, she said she was heading to Lavish to pick up breakfast."

"How long she been gone?"

"A little over an hour."

"Fuck."

"Is something wrong?"

"Did you see anybody with her or around her?"

"No sir, she was alone."

"Call me the second she walks through the door."

"Yes sir.

I hung up and called Mo again, but she still didn't answer so I pulled up the tracking device that solo put on her phone. The second the location showed up, I knew something was wrong. I immediately went to the closet, opened my floor safe, and got my gun out. Mo was missing, and I knew who had her.

"Los has Mo," I said the second I heard my brother's voice.

"The fuck you mean Los has Mo!"

"You heard me. He has her. I woke up this morning and she was gone. Davis said she left to get breakfast an hour ago, and she's not back yet. I tracked her phone and it showed up. She doesn't even know where the fuck that is."

"Where are you?"

"I'm leaving my place right now."

"Where are you going?"

"The fuck you think? I'm going to get her and then I'm killing that muthafucker."

"Calm your ass down for a minute and let me think."

"Fuck you Kay. I don't have a minute. If he lays his hands on her, I swear I kill his whole fucking family."

"Look, you're not going after Los by yourself. It's what he wants so that's a stupid move. You're acting off emotion right now and you of all people know better than that. You're gonna fuck around and not only get yourself killed but Mo too. Is that what you want, Karter? I was on my way to King's. Meet me there and we'll get her back, but we're doing this shit together."   I didn't respond, because everything in me was telling me fuck everything and to just go get Mo.

"Karter, do you fucking hear me?" Kay yelled.

"Yeah muthafucker I hear you, but you better hurry the fuck up because if I get to Kings before you do, then I'm doing this shit on my own."

On the way to King's house, I tried Mo several more times but she didn't answer. It just rang and then went to voicemail. I knew she was still alive, for now anyway, because Los wanted me and he was using Mo to make that happen. The problem was that I didn't know what he would do to her while he had her, and that shit was fucking with me.

When I pulled up at King's house, Kay's car was there along with Shine and Royal's, so I got out and King opened the front door the second I hit the steps. He was dressed in all black, so I already knew where his mind was. I walked inside, and Royal, Shine, and Kay were all dressed in black, waiting. The second I stepped in the kitchen, my phone went off.

"Mo where are you?" As soon as I said her name, all eyes were on me.

"Just listen," Mo said. I could tell she was crying, which sent fire through my veins. "He knows you're tracking me, so he knows you're coming."

"Is he there with you now?"

"I'm here and I'll see you soon bitch, come and get me," Los said, and then hung up on me.

"What did she say?" Kay asked as he walked up to me.

"I'm out. If you're rolling with me then let's go, but I don't have time for bullshit right now." I turned to leave, and heard King behind me.

"Let's do this shit." I climbed in my car with Kay in the passenger seat, while Royal and Shine got in with King.

Somebody was going to die tonight. I just hoped it wasn't one of us.

Kay

I kept watching my brother as he dashed in and out of traffic. Karter was in a zone, and he was out for blood. I knew the look he had in his eyes, and it was one that ended in someone losing their live. When he got like this, his emotions were cut off, ice ran through his veins, and he functioned like a machine. He had transformed himself into a killer, and he was not going to stop until his target was dead.

"Karter, you good?" I glanced at my brother again, and his eyes met mine. He didn't say a word; he just nodded and then let his eyes fall on the road again.

Shit was all kinds of messed up right now, and I knew that Karter had one goal in mind, and that was to get Mo and kill Los. He couldn't and wouldn't focus on anything else until he knew that she was safe.

We pulled up a few blocks away from the warehouse, but could see several cars parked outside of it. Karter and I got out, followed by King, Royal, and Shine. Right after, I noticed a jeep pull up behind King, and he walked right to it while I just watched until La stepped out the driver's side with Blaze and Soonie with her.

"Yo, what up La," King said.

He dapped Blaze and Soonie before they made their way over to us. Karter still hadn't said a word; he just opened his trunk and lifted the baseboard, pulling out two Choppers. He handed me one, and then leaned the other against his car.

"So what's the plan?" Royal asked, now focused on Karter. Karter made sure his guns were loaded, and then handed me a clip.

"Kill everything moving and make sure we get Mo out of there," Karter said without looking up.

"I can fucks with that, but I figured you had some strategical shit worked out," Royal said, eyeing Karter.

"We don't have time for that shit," King said.

"I'm just asking, you know how that muthafucker was in SC. He had that shit all mapped out in his head and shit, but I'm ready for whatever."

"You got the vests?" King asked Blaze.

"Yeah we're good on that." Blaze walked around to the back of La's Jeep and pulled the rear door open. He started handing out vests, and everyone grabbed one except Karter. I knew he wasn't going to wear that shit, so I didn't even asked.

"We ready?" I asked, looking around at our team.

"Hell yeah, let's fuck some shit up," Shine said.

"They know we're coming, so they're waiting. Just shoot everything moving and try not to get shot," Karter said, and as everyone started moving to the warehouse, he grabbed my arm.

"Stay with me," he said, giving me the most serious look.

"The fuck you think I am Karter? I know how to handle myself." I hated when he pulled that big brother shit.

"I know you do muthafucker, but this shit right here is on me and if anybody's catching a bullet today, it will only be me. Not you, so calm your ass down and stay with me."

"Yeah whatever muthafucker, let's go." I snatched away from him and caught up with the rest of the team. I knew Karter felt like this shit was his fault, but we weren't ten years old anymore. I had to make my own decisions and deal with the consequences, and today wasn't going to be any different.

"They don't have cameras, so as soon as we hit the door just start shooting. He won't have Mo out in the open, but just be careful," Karter said as we all posted up outside the door.

He pushed the oversized metal door and stepped inside, with me right behind him. La's gangster ass was right beside me while King, Royal, and Shine were covering us. The seconded we stepped foot in the warehouse, bullets started flying.

Karter's dumb ass walked right into the middle of it, taking shots one after another, and that shit had me fucking amazed. I knew my brother was good at what he did but his ass fired, dropping each target with one shot to the head without even flinching. The rest of us fired, dodging bullets while Karter's ass kept moving straight through the building, like there weren't bullets flying past his ass and shit. It was like he was a machine. Zoned out. I had never seen anything like that before.

After we had literally dropped everyone in the room, Karter walked over to one of the guys who had only been caught in the side, but dude scrambled for his gun until Karter shot him in the leg. Karter yanked him off the floor and looked him right in the eyes.

"Tell me where she is and I won't finish you off." Dude looked at Karter for a second, as if debating whether or not he was going to tell, but when he felt Karter's gun in his chest he started talking.

"Upstairs in the office," he said through clenched teeth, trying to mask the pain of his wounds.   Karter glanced at me, and I shot dude in the head.

"Damn, you told that nigga you weren't going to kill his ass," Royal said and then laughed.

"I didn't," Karter said before he released dude, whose body hit the ground.

"Yo, are we all good?" King asked, looking around at everyone.

"I think I caught one, but I'm good," Soonie said, lifting his vest.

"Take him outside. We've got this." I looked around and there had to be at least ten bodies on the floor, so I was guessing that there couldn't be many more to handle.

"Aight bet." Blaze put his arm around Soonie and helped him out the door.

"I'm staying," La said before she stared looking around.

"We're going to check out the rest of the place. Go get your girl," King said, nodding to Karter.

He and I took off towards the stairs; Karter went first with no signs of anyone around, so I followed with my gun in hand, looking around. Once we were up the stairs and moving towards the direction of the office, a shot was fired but Karter pointed, aimed, and a body dropped right in front of us. Karter nodded towards the office door, which was open, and he and I both posted up against the wall outside of it before Karter peeked around the corner.

"Come on in. We've been waiting." I assumed it was Los, because Karter pulled his body from the wall and stepped inside with his gun aimed. I was right behind him and knew that shit was about to get bad. Los was standing in the middle of the room with his arm around Mo's waist. She was naked, and he had his gun pointed at her stomach.

"She and I had a little fun while we were waiting on you. Didn't we, Mo?" Los kissed her on her cheek, and a tear slid down her face. Her eyes stayed focused on Karter, aside from the brief second that she laid eyes on me.

"You're a bitch, just like I always knew you were. Why didn't you just come after me like a real man," Karter said.

"Because I wanted to taste this pussy one last time before I killed her and this bastard baby," Los said with a cocky grin. I could see Karter out the corner of my eye, and he tightened the grip on his gun.

"Let her go. You want me, you've got me. Don't be a fucking bitch." Los laughed and let his gun slide down Mo's stomach before he aimed it right at her.

"Are you worried, Karter? You weren't worried when you were fucking my bitch, so why are you worried now?"

"I'm going to say this one last time. Let her go."

"Or what, are you going to-"

I felt a bullet fly by me, and it pierced Los right in the head. He hit the floor, and Mo screamed as Karter ran to her and wrapped her his arms. I looked back, and King was standing in the doorway holding his gun. Karter looked up and nodded at him before he pulled off his shirt and pulled it over Mo's head.

Karter lifted Mo off the ground and carried her out of the warehouse straight to his car. The job was done, and everyone went their separate ways while Karter and I took Mo back to his apartment.

*****

"How is she?" I could see the stress all over my brother's face as he walked out of his bedroom into the kitchen. He grabbed two beers before he joined me in the living room, sat down across from me, and handed me one. He let his head fall back as he turned up his beer and damn near finished the whole thing, and then sat it on the table in front of him.

"Shit, I don't know. She hasn't really said anything."

"Just give her a minute," I said. Mo loved Karter and I knew that she wouldn't bail on him, even after everything that happened.

"All I keep thinking about is what he did to her. That shit has got my head so fucked up that I can't even think straight."

"You're gonna have to figure out how to let that shit go, Karter. She needs you right now, and she can read you better than anybody. No matter what it takes, you better figure out a way to let that shit go and be whatever she needs you to be."

I knew my brother. He felt think this was his fault and that he let her down, but Mo knew the risk of dealing with Karter. As fucked up as it was, she had to consider the possibility that something like this could happen, but I understood how Karter felt. If it had been Lane, I would have been the same way-ready to fuck shit up and kill everything moving-but Los was dead, and whoever was left standing on his team wouldn't dare come at us without a leader, so shit should be getting back to normal soon. All Karter needed to do now was be there for Mo.

When I finally made it home, I was tired as hell and just ready to lay up under Lane. We had been through so much in the past twelve hours that I just needed a minute to press pause.

"Hey babe, how is she?" The second I walked in my bedroom and laid eyes on Lane, everything instantly felt better. She was here, safe at my house, in my bed, and that shit just felt right. It had a nigga trying to hide his smile.

Lane climbed off the bed, wearing some little ass shorts that I could barely see and one of my t-shirts, which immediately had my body reacting. She made her way over to me and wrapped her arms around me, resting her head on my chest.

"It's hard to say right now. Karter said she hasn't said much." I leaned down and kissed Lane on the neck before I stepped away and started coming out of my clothes.

"I want to go see her, but she probably doesn't want to see anybody right now. I just want her to know that we're here for her."

When I looked at Lane, I could see the compassion in her eyes, which was cute. She had such a good heart and I loved that about her. A lot of it came from the fact that she went through so much with Dez, but all and all she was just a good person.

After I stripped down to my boxers, I walked up to Lane and pulled her into a kiss before I let her go just enough to see her face.

"She knows. She's just not in a good place right now, but she'll be alright."

Lane looked up at me and frowned. She was so damn beautiful that I could look at her all day every day, and never get tired. Lane had a softness about her that made you want to protect her, but then she was also a fighter.

"I missed you today," Lane said with a devilish grin before she pulled her shirt over her head and tossed it on the bed. Her full perky breasts had my mouth watering just looking at them.

"Oh yeah?" I asked as she slid her yoga shorts down her thighs, and then stepped out of them.

"Yeah," she said as she bit her bottom lip and stared at me.

"What are you doing?" I asked as I pulled her into my chest again and leaned down to kiss her on the neck.

"We're taking a shower," she said as she let her hands slide up my back, and then pulled away. She left me standing there and walked into the bathroom. A few seconds later, I heard the shower running and followed her.

Lane let her thong hit the floor, and I did the same with my boxers before I opened the glass door and waited for her to step inside. I was right behind her, shutting it after I was inside.

"Don't get my hair wet, Kayman," Lane said as she stepped under the water, keeping enough distance so that her hair wasn't at risk. I just laughed and forced her back against the wall.

"I can't promise you that."

I kissed Lane so deep that I felt like she was draining every bit of energy I had left in my body. When I finally came up for air, she had a huge grin on her face.

"I guess you missed me too," she said

"Little bit," I couldn't control my smile.

My hand found her center and once my fingers were inside, I used my thumb to massage her swollen clit, causing Lane to let out a few soft moans before I began gently sucking her neck.

"How much did you miss me, Laney?" I whispered against her ear.

"A lot." Her breathing was labored, and she tightened her grip on my arms. I just smiled, knowing that she was about to cum.

"Let it go, Laney." I covered her lips with mine, and applied more pressure to her clit. She released our kiss, bit down on her bottom lip, and came so hard that she had to hold on to me to keep her balance.

"Turn around," I said as I let my arm slide around her waist, pulling her back just enough for her to lean slightly forward. When I entered her, she reached back and gripped my thigh, trying to control the pain, but I didn't give in. I went so deep that she could barely keep up as I moved inside her.

"Shit Laney. You got a nigga about to lose it." I bit down on her shoulder the deeper I went, trying my best to control what I was feeling, but it was too late. Fuck it. We were gonna have to have a round two later. I gripped Lane's waist hard as hell and went in, and we came together. With my body pressed firmly against hers, we both stood there out of breath.

"That shit doesn't make no sense," I laughed as I stepped up under the shower head, letting the water run over my head and down my body.

"What?" Lane asked as she wrapped her arms around my waist, pressing her chest against my back. She reached down and let her hands slide up and down my shaft, causing it to stand at attention.

"You're trying to send a brother to the emergency room with that shit you got between your legs, and you better chill with that before I have your ass unable to walk tomorrow." I knocked her hand away and pushed her away from my body. She just laughed before she grabbed her body wash and loofa.

"I love you, Kayman." Lane was behind me, but I could hear the smile in her voice.

"Shit you better. I'm the truth girl."

"Let's try that again, I love you Kayman."

"I turned and pulled her into a kiss. "I love you too. You already know."

Shine

"What?" I yelled into my phone. I didn't even bother checking to see who was calling. My damn head was pounding, and I still felt the three bottles of Ciroc that I drank.

"Can you, Can you...oh shit!" I held my phone away from my face to see who the fuck was yelling in my ear.

"Asia, the fuck is wrong with you?"

"I'm in labor asshole. Will you come to the hospital?" she yelled, sobering my ass up real quick.

"Where are you?"

"Duke Labor and Delivery...fuck!" she yelled. She was breathing hard as hell, and she sounded crazy as fuck.

"Yeah, I'll be there."

"Shit," I mumbled as I sat up and massaged my temples. It was four in the morning, and I was likely still drunk as hell. Why the fuck couldn't babies come during normal business hours? What the hell was wrong with a 9 to 5 delivery time?

I stood up, opened my drawer, and grabbed a t-shirt. I pulled it over my head, walked into our guest bedroom, and stood in the door way watching Meka sleep. Damn I loved her ass, and shit was about to get real fucking complicated.

She had been home for three weeks after she walked out on my ass. Things were extremely tense between us, but she was trying and I loved her for that. She was home, but she wasn't fucking with me for the most part, but I had her home and that was good enough for me. For right now.

I walked in room and sat on the bed next to her before I reached under the covers and placed my hand on her stomach. I couldn't wait to meet my son. I had a love for him that couldn't be explained, and he wasn't even here yet.

That was the shit that pissed me off about Asia. If that baby turned out to really be mine, I would have to grow to love her. There wasn't any type of connection there, and honestly that shit didn't seem real to me. But this right here, this baby growing in Meka was real as fuck. He was mine, and I could feel that shit in my soul.

I leaned down and kissed the side of Meka's face, and she swatted me away before she snuggled close to me. She was asleep, so she had no idea what she was doing because I could guarantee that she didn't want to be anywhere near my ass right now.

"Meek, wake up baby," I placed my hand on the side of her face and let my thumb slide across her jawline. I hated to do this shit, but she wanted to be there when Asia had the baby and I made her a promise that she could be.

"Mmmm, what time is it?" she mumbled, still half asleep.

"It's after four, Asia's in labor."

Meka's eyes popped open, and she snatched away from me and sat up. I just stared at her for a second as her expression dropped and she looked at me. Hurt filled her eyes, and that shit had a nigga feeling like the enemy.

"You said you wanted to be there," I said to break the silence.

"No Stanly, I said I didn't want you to go alone. I don't want to fucking be there while your bitch is possibly having your baby."

"Meek, I know you don't want to hear this shit again but I'm sorry. If I could take that it back then I would, but I can't baby and I'm sorry."

"It's fine. Just leave so I can get dressed," she said, and then climbed out the other side of the bed.

She was pissed and hurting, and there wasn't shit I could do about it. To make matters worse, if the baby did end up being mine then I wasn't sure that we would make it. I didn't know if she would stick around for that.

An hour later, we were at the hospital and shit went bad from the second I stepped foot on the floor. Asia's sister walked right up to me, yelling about how I was less of a man because I made her go through the pregnancy alone, while her mother was yelling at me because Meka was with me.

"You're a real asshole. You know that?" Asia's mother yelled.

"With all due respect, you can be mad all you want but I don't recall laying between your legs, so as far as I'm concerned your opinion don't mean shit to me, so get the fuck out of my face with all that," I yelled back as I took Meka's hand and walked into the waiting room.

"She's in labor about to have your daughter, and you can't even go in there and help her through it." Her sister was standing in front of me with her arms crossed, glaring at Meka.

"First off all, I don't know if that damn baby is mine, but if she is then I'll deal with that. As for being in there with her, I'm good on that shit. She didn't give a shit about me being a part of this process for the past eight months, so there's no need for me to jump in there now. Why don't you take your ass in there instead of standing out her in my face and if you keep looking at my girl like that you gon' make me fuck your ass up, so go on with that shit."

I put my arm around Meka's shoulder and she let me, but her body was stiff as a board. I didn't give a fuck though; I was just glad that she let me get that close to her.

"Fuck you, Shine. I swear to God if that baby is yours, you're going to pay."

"What the fuck ever. Just get out of my face."

Melissa stormed off with her mother right behind her, and the second they were out of sight

Meka pulled away from me. I leaned back and closed my eyes. I was just ready for this shit to be over.

What seemed like days later, but in reality was only hours later, Melissa was standing in front of me mugging me hard as hell. Meka was asleep on the sofa next to me with her head resting on my lap.

"Hey asshole, your daughter is here if you want to see her. Everything went fine, she's healthy and Asia's good too, by the way."

"Man fuck you," I yelled, causing Meka to sit up and rub her eyes.

"I'll be right back." I walked out of the waiting room straight to the nurse's station.

"I need a paternity test done on the baby in room 302. I've got cash right now. I'll pay whatever it costs, and I need that shit back as soon as you can get it."

"Sir, we can schedule the test, but you'll have to go to accounting to pay for it," she smiled at me.

"Fine, just do whatever so I can take my ass home," I said.

An hour later, I was out of 800 dollars and in my car on my way home. Meka was quiet as hell, but I knew she was hurt. The baby was here and we would know in 24 hours if she was mine. That shit was weighing heavy on both of us. Talk about a fucking elephant in the room.

It was almost 10:00 when we got home, and I was tired as fuck. All I wanted to do was take my ass to sleep, but I couldn't because I kept thinking about how my life was about to change if that baby was mine.

After I had the house locked up and checked all the security cameras, I went in our room, undressed, and climbed into bed. The second I closed my eyes, I heard Meka's voice from the door.

"Why didn't you want to see her...the baby?"

"I just don't until I know whether or not she's really mine," I said truthfully. There was no reason to open that door until I knew for sure.

Meka stood there for a minute before she walked into our bedroom. She stood next to the bed, and I could tell that she wanted to say something but she didn't; she just stood there looking at me.

"What's on your mind, Meek?" I stared her deep in her eyes and waited.

"Can I lay down with you for a little while?"

I chuckled. "Meka, this is your bed and I'm your man. You don't have to ask me that shit."

I pulled the covers back and held my arm out. Meka looked down at my body, realizing I only had on boxer briefs, but she should have already known that shit. She knew me. Meka climbed into bed with me and snuggled close to my body. I wrapped my arms around her and rested my chin on her shoulder.

"I hate you for this," Meka said softly.

"I know, and I'm sorry."

"You keep saying that, but it doesn't change anything."

"I don't know what else to say, Meek. I fucked up. I really fucked up."

"What if I can't handle it?" Meka sounded like she was about to cry.

"We'll figure it out. I promise. I'm gonna make this shit up to you. I don't know how, but I will. Just don't leave me."

Meka didn't say anything else, and neither did I. We had both been up for hours, and I just wanted to go to sleep with my baby in my arms and pretend like everything was back the way it used to be, before Asia showed up.

*****

I opened my eyes and stretched, still feeling like shit. Meka was asleep next to me, so I carefully moved away from her, stood up, and grabbed my phone. It was just after 3:00, which meant that we had both been sleep for a few hours. I had my phone on silent because I didn't want to be bothered, so I had ten missed calls from Asia and one from Royal.

I wasn't in the mood to deal with Asia; in fact, I didn't have shit to say to her until the results came back. The hospital had my number, so they were going to call me as soon as the results were back, so Asia could kiss my ass for now. I decided to call Royal back to make sure nothing was going down.

"I called your ass two hours ago, where the fuck you been?" Royal's bipolar ass yelled as soon as he answered.

"Home muthafucker. I just woke up. Asia had the baby last night."

"Word? How did that shit go?" I stood up and walked out of the room, closing the door behind me. I walked through my house until I made it to the kitchen and pulled the refrigerator open.

"How the fuck you think that shit went? Meka is mad as hell and hurt, while Asia is still on my dick."

I smiled when I had to move the apple juice around to find a bottle of water. Meka was living off that shit, and we currently had four containers of it taking up all the space.

"Damn bruh, that's a fucked up situation but that shit will work itself out, and if not your ass is just gonna be broke as fuck paying child support and shit for two kids."

"Fuck you Royal. Why the hell did you call me?"

"You know I'm just fucking with you. Meka will be alright. She loves your dusty ass, so she's not going anywhere. That shit is just heavy, so she needs a minute."

"I know she's not going anywhere. I would lock her ass in one of these damn guest rooms if I had to. I'm talking straight up Dateline Mystery."

"Nigga don't let me see your ass on no damn Dateline, and I mean that shit," Royal said, and then laughed.

"Aye, I'm keeping my family together by all means necessary." Now I was laughing.

"Yo, I'm not fucking with you like that but real talk, we're hitting up Silhouette tonight. You down?"

"Hell no, Meka already hates my ass. The last thing I need is to be up in a damn strip club."

"Meka will be at King's house tonight. With everything going on, Free wanted to get all the girls together, so we're heading out. We need that shit, man. We've been stressed as hell dealing with all the shit going."

"I'll let you know."

"Aight bet, but I'm out. I have to spend some time with Lace so she won't flip the fuck out on me later about this shit."

"Damn muthafucker, it's like that?" I just laughed. His dumb ass must really be in love if he's worried about Lace's reaction to him going to a strip club. Hell, Silhouette used to be his second home. I think his ass had a room set up in that bitch, real talk.

"Hell yeah it's like that. You know Lace is insane, and I don't have time to be in jail for fucking her little ass up." He sounded serious as hell, which made me laugh.

"Aight well I'm out, so I'll hit you up later."

"Aight bet."

"Who was that?" I turned around when I heard Meka's voice

"Royal." I wanted to smile, because she looked cute as hell in a pair of leggings and a V-neck tee that hugged her body. Meka was already thick before she got pregnant, but the baby had her breasts and ass hypnotizing a brother.

"I think I'm hanging out with Free tonight," she said as she walked past me. "She just called and said she wants everyone to chill at her house tonight."

I kept my eyes on her as she moved around the kitchen, but she never would look at me other than a brief glance. This shit was killing me, but I knew there wasn't anything I could do about it. Meka opened the refrigerator to put the apple juice back in, and I walked up behind her and placed my hands on her stomach.

"I know hate me right now and shit is all kinds of fucked up, but I swear on everything that I will make this right. I don't know how, but I will.

Just don't give up on me." Her body was tense, but she relaxed a little when I kissed her on the neck.

"I can't promise you that, but I'm trying." She pulled away from me, picked up her glass, and then left the kitchen.

All I could do was stand there and watch her walk away. This shit was all on me.

Free

I had just finished getting dressed for my six-week checkup, and was on my way downstairs to get Mani from Diego so that I could get her changed and ready to go. I swear, she had Diego under her spell and it was the most adorable thing ever. I loved the way he loved her, even though it had me feeling a little jealous from time to time. It was all good though, because Diego made sure I knew he loved me just as much.

"You need to finish getting dressed so we can leave," I said as I approached Diego to take Imani from him. He had her tucked in one arm while he was flipping through what looked like bank deposits with the other. He looked up at me and smile.

"What time is it?"

"Almost ten something and my appointment is at 11:15."

Diego lifted Imani and kissed both of her chubby little cheeks before he handed her too me. I smiled a little, because they looked like twins with all that wild curly hair. She looked just like him.

"Why the hell you grinning like that, Free?" Diego asked after he stood up and wrapped his arms around me."

"Nothing," I said.

"It must be something if you're cheesing and shit." Just as he said, that Imani looked up at me and smiled.

"See, you even got her little ass smiling and shit."

"You've got problems Dey, go get dressed so we can go," I said, and pulled away from him. We both left his office and half an hour later, were sitting at my doctor's office waiting on Dr. Lennox.

"You know if she doesn't tell me what I wanna hear we're getting a second opinion, right?" Diego looked up from his phone briefly and then went back to checking his messages.

"Like what?" I asked, not understanding what he meant.

"That you're ready for sex. Shit, it's been six weeks Free, and I need that shit."

"I looked at Diego and rolled my eyes. "You can't just get a second opinion, Dey. It doesn't work like that."

"Yes hell it does, shit it better because if she doesn't give you the green light, then I'm getting a second, a third, hell we'll hit up every damn doctor in the state until one of the bitches says I can be up in them guts."

Diego tried his best to keep a straight face, but the longer he looked at me, he began to smile until he started laughing.

"You are so damn stupid," I said, unable to control my laughter.

"That's not stupid, that's called desperate." Diego kissed me before he bent over to grab the pacifier that Imani spit out.

"Free Evans," the nurse called my name, and looked around the waiting room until I stood, and then she focused on me with a smile. Diego stood up and was about to grab Imani's carrier, but I stopped him.

"You can wait here. She's just going to do an exam and then ask me a few questions."

"Nah, fuck that. I need to be in there to make sure she knows how important this is," Dey said before he grabbed the handle of Imani's carrier and followed behind me.

After we were in the exam room, I was undressed and on the table as Diego sat in the corner with Imani in his arms while we waited for Dr. Lennox. It felt so strange being in there with him. I quickly learned that being naked in front of a man for the purpose of sex and being naked while waited to be examined by your doctor were two completely different feelings. It was awkward enough going through it any way, and Dey being in there wasn't helping the situation.

There was a knock on the door, and then it opened with Dr. Lennox smiling as she entered the room.

"Hello Free, how's everything going?" she asked as she placed her clipboard on the counter, and then made her way over to Diego.

"Is this our little angel?" Dr. Lennox said as she looked down at Imani lying peacefully in Diego's arms.

"I see she's got dad's hair," she said as she smiled at him, and then focused on me.

"So Free, how are you feeling?"

"Pretty good I guess." Hell I had never had a baby before, so as far as I could tell things were good. Dr. Lennox opened the draw to get a pair of latex gloves. She pulled them on and then sat down on the rolling stool next to my exam table.

"So any discomfort?"

"Nope, everything seems fine," I said.

"Well, let's just take a look and make sure," Dr. Lennox said.

"Yeah, let's make sure all her shit is in working order," Diego said.

"Dey!" I yelled before I turned my head and narrowed my eyes at him. I couldn't believe this fool was in here talking so crazy.

Dr. Lennox just laughed and then focused on me. "Well, I guess I have my marching order. Let's get started." I just shook my head and scooted to the end of the table. I swear, I if I could have reached my gun I would have shot his inconsiderate behind.

An hour later, we were in Diego's truck and on our way to Sage House. Diego was happy as hell, because apparently all my parts were in working order again.

"Let me see her," Tish said the second we hit the front door. Diego sat Imani's carrier on the bar, and Tish immediately began unbuckling her so that she could get her out.

"Oh my God she is beautiful, Free," Tish said after she had Imani in her arms.

"Thanks Tish," I beamed.

"Even though she looks like a little mini me for King with all this damn hair." She looked up at Dey and frowned.

"You damn right that's my little mini me," Dey said.

Tish ignored Diego and walked into the restaurant carrying Imani, so I grabbed her carrier and followed behind her.

"Is she a good baby?" Tish asked looking up at me after we got comfy in one of the booths.

"Yeah, she really is. She's already basically sleeping through the night."

"Dang girl. Landon is almost six and he's still not sleeping through the night."

I guess I just got lucky."

"And I hate you, by the way. You don't even look like you had a baby, Free. That's not right," Tish rolled her eyes at me.

"Trust me, I feel like it, though."

After word got out that Dey and I had the baby with us, most of the staff stopped by our table to see her, and Ronnie finally surfaced. After he took our orders, he leaned over Tish, who refused to let Imani go to get a better look at her before he turned to me and smiled.

"She's beautiful, Free." I smiled and said thank you, but Diego had to have a say in it.

"Damn, can I get a *congrats King*?" he playfully mugged Ronnie, and then Tish. "You know she didn't do that shit all by herself."

"Whatever King, did you carry a baby for nine months and then go through labor, feeling like your body was being ripped apart? No you didn't." Tish turned away from King and looked at me. "So congrats Free, she's beautiful."

"Man fuck that, I don't know what you learned in school but I know for sure it takes it two to make a baby."

"Just like a man. Trying to take credit for everything," Tish said and rolled her eyes at Diego, making me and Ronnie both laugh.

"Damn Ronnie, you're supposed to be on my side," Diego said.

"You're on your own with that, King. I have a wife and three children. I know better. Choose your battles man," Ronnie said just before he left us at the table.

Diego just shook his head and laughed. He knew he was out numbered, so he just let it go.

*****

I watched as Diego came stepping out of the closet, looking good as always, dressed in jeans and a button up Polo shirt. He had just showered, so his scent filled the room as he moved around getting ready to leave.

I was sitting in the center of our bed watching TV while I waited for my girls to show up, and Diego was about to head out to meet the guys for a night out at Silhouette. I wasn't thrilled about it, but I wasn't going to trip either. I trusted him.

"You better behave tonight," I said as I looked up from the TV long enough to catch his eye. A smirk spread across his face as he moved to the foot of the bed and folded his arms.

"I better," he questioned, like he found my statement amusing.

"Yeah, you better," I said firmly.

He let out a cocky laugh, "and if I don't?"

"Trust me, you just better," I said, and mugged him hard as hell.

125

He crawled onto the bed with me and pulled me by the waist so that I was on my back, and he was hovering over me.

"So you call yourself bossing up on me?" he said, looking down at me with a grin.

"Call it what you what, just make sure you don't get confused about where home is while you're out tonight." Diego just smiled at me as he used his hand to spread my legs apart.

"Trust me, I know where home is and there is no confusion about that." He let his hand move into my yoga shorts and began massaging my center as he leaned down to kiss me. After a few minutes, he pulled away with a smirk.

"Yeah, I think all your parts are in working order again. Be naked when I get home tonight. We've got a lot of catching up to do." Diego kissed me on the neck before he climbed off the bed, and then went into the bathroom.

There was no doubt about it; I was most definitely going to be ready and waiting for Diego when he got home tonight.

"Aye boo," Lane said as she knocked and walked into our bedroom, and went straight to Imani's bassinet. When she realized she wasn't in there, she frowned.

"Where's my baby?"

"In her room sleep, and do not bother her," I said firmly.

"Well damn, look who decided to show their face," Diego said the second he laid eyes on Lane.

"Shut up, King. You see me all the time," she said with a grin before she climbed on the bed next to me and leaned back against the headboard.

"I've seen the back your damn head as you walked out the door, but that's about it."

"Awe King, you miss me?"

"Hell no. I'm just trying to make sure Kay don't have you locked in the basement or some crazy shit like that."

Lane just laughed. "You're so damn stupid. Why would he lock me in the basement?"

"Shit you never know, your ass might be acting up."

"Dey really?" I shook my head and laughed.

"Hell yeah. You better be naked when I get home or your ass might end up locked in the damn basement too," Diego winked at me.

"I guess you heard that, Free."

"Don't let his crazy ass fool you. He knows better." Diego walked to the side of the bed and kissed me on the cheek before he moved towards the door.

"She's just talking shit, Lane. Free knows what's up. I'm out."

A few minutes later, I heard the alarm announce that the front door was open and, then I heard Diego talking to someone before he yelled my name. Lane and I climbed off the bed and when I reached the top of the stairs, I saw Mo was here, so we headed down to meet her.

"What's up girl, you look good," I said before I hugged her, and when I released her Lane hugged her too. This was the first time I had been around Mo since the whole Los thing. We had talked on the phone, but she hadn't really been out since that situation went down.

Mo looked flawless, which I was sure had to do with the fact that she was a model and used to always being in the public eye. Her short, cropped hair was wrapped and pushed off her face, while she wore a cream sweater smock with dark grey leggings and black ankle boots.

"Where's Lace and Meka?" she asked after we walked into the living room and got comfortable.

"On their way," I said as I pulled my feet up and crossed my legs so that I was sitting Indian style. Lane was stretched out on the chaise, while Mo sat on the sofa across from me.

"I'm glad you're here," Lane said, smiling at Mo.

"Me too. I needed to get out of that apartment. Karter has been hovering so much that it is starting to drive me a little crazy. I know he's worried about me, but him asking me all day if I'm okay only reminds me about why he's asking."

"Kay was like that with me after the whole Dez thing. He would literally ask me every ten minutes and it drove me crazy, but it's just because they're so used to controlling everything that when they can't they feel helpless. When stuff happens to us that they can't control, then it's like they don't know how to function, but it's all out of love."

Mo smiled, "I know, which is why I just let it go but I needed this. I needed to get away from a minute and not think about it."

"Front door open."

I looked up when I heard the alarm, and a few minute later Meka and Lace joined us.

"Dang, why you sitting in her looking all sad? We're supposed to be chilling tonight," Lace said as she surveyed our faces.

"Girl shut up, we're not sad."

"Good, because I didn't come here for all that," Lace said, and then sat down next to Mo while Meka sat down next to me.

"What time are the strippers coming?" Lane asked as she looked around at all of us with a grin.

"You're joking right?" I said. "You know damn well that's not happening up in this house."

129

Meka laughed. "Girl, King would lose his damn mind."

"Strippers?" Mo asked, looking confused.

"Long story, boo," Meka said.

"Do I even want to know?" Mo asked.

"Nah, not really," I said.

We all spent the next few hour laughing and talking about everything but our problems. Mo had one night where she didn't have to think about Los, and Meka got to let go of the fact that Shine possibly had another baby out there. We just laughed and joked and enjoyed our much needed girl time.

King

Me and my people were set up in VIP chillin. The club was packed as usual, and we had all eyes on us. We were all feeling nice, but not so much that we weren't aware of our surroundings. All of our current beefs were settled, and it felt good as hell to just be out without looking over our shoulders. We still had to be cautious, just because of who we were, but for the first time in a long time, I felt like I could actually relax a little, and it felt good.

"Yo, this shit is wild tonight," Karter said as he turned up a bottle of Hennessey he was holding and sat down next to me.

"Yeah, they're doing their thing," I said looking around. All the baddest strippers were in VIP with us, which was to be expected since our pockets were deep and they were hoping for the chance of getting a little more from us than just a few stacks. Karter sat his empty bottle down on the table in front of us and started grinning.

"I'm drunk as hell," he said, and then laughed.

"Yes you are," I just shook my head, because he was. Karter was a lot like Royal, though. They were functioning, alcoholics so they could be drunk as shit and still be able to maintain.

"Hey sexy. Why are you sitting over here all alone?" I looked up just as one of the girls found her way onto my lap and let her hands move down my chest.

"I'm just chillin," I said as she got comfortable and I wrapped my arm around her waist, letting my hand rest on her thigh.

"You're too sexy to be alone, though."

"Oh yeah, why is that?" I asked. She leaned into my chest and let her lips graze the side of my face.

"Because it's a shame for all this sexy to be on display without putting it to good use."

She pulled back and looked at me seductively before she reached down and began to rub my dick. I had to admit, she was well worth looking at, but I wasn't crossing that line with anybody tonight. Being here right now was just foreplay until I could get home and get in between Free's legs.

"I guess it will just have to be a waste then," I said, grabbing her wrist and pulling it away from me.

She smiled at me before she leaned in again, "Don't worry, I don't kiss and tell."

I just laughed. "I'm not worried. I'm a grown ass man and I make my own decisions, but you sweetheart, are not what I want."

She snatched away from me and grabbed my dick again. "Are you sure about that?"

"Without a doubt." I grabbed her roughly around her waist so that she understood that I meant business, and then I forced her off my lap. When she was on her feet, she narrowed her eyes at me.

"Fuck you," she said as she turned to leave, and Roz walked in right behind her.

"King, are you not playing nice," Roz said as she sat down on Karter's lap and let her hand run across his head and down the back of his neck.

I just chuckled. "Come on Roz, you know me, I always play nice."

She smiled before she turned to Karter. "You look like you're feeling good, Karter."

"Hell yeah I am. Real good." Karter leaned forward and grabbed a few bills off one of the stacks of cash we had siting on the table in front of us, and tucked them into Roz's thong.

"Now go play. I'm on a *look but don't touch* policy tonight," Karter said as he smiled at Roz.

"I hope your women appreciate what they have, because if not I promise I can show them how to."

Roz stood up and walked behind the sofa we were sitting on before she let her hand go through my hair. She leaned down and kissed me on the neck before she walked out of VIP. "Have fun guys," she said, and blew a kiss at me and Karter.

"The fuck is your problem? Last I checked you weren't part of my team, so keep your fucking eyes out of VIP!" Royal yelled at some dude who was sitting at a table just outside of our section.

I stood up, followed by Karter and Kay, while Shine was already bossed up next to Royal.

"Melanie, let's go. Fuck this shit. Your ass is only supposed to be on the stage anyway," Dude said, addressing one of the girls that were in VIP with us tending to Royal.

"I knew you couldn't handle this shit, Mike. You need to just leave. I'm trying to do my job."

"Yeah Mike, she's trying to do her fucking job," Royal said before he grabbed the girl's ass and pulled her into his body.

"Ah fuck. Here we go," Karter mumbled as he and I stood, watching to see how this was going to turn out.

At this point, it was so loud and wild in the club that no one was really paying attention to what was going on.

"Melanie, I'm not gonna tell your dumb ass again. Get your ass out here and let's go." He moved near the waist high wall that separated VIP from the rest of the club, but he kept his eyes on his girl. I guess she didn't want to create a problem, because she tried to move away from Royal.

"Nah ma, we're busy. That muthafucker can wait," Royal said. He was drunk as hell, and I knew that he wasn't going to let that shit go.

"Royal, let her go before we have to beat dude's ass. I'm trying to have a good time tonight, not knock a muthafucker out," Kay said.

"Fuck you, bitch. Just because you're throwing money around in here don't mean shit. Money don't make you hard," Dude said, no longer focused on Kay.

"Yo Mike, what up, you good?" Two of his so-called homeboys were now beside him giving him instant courage but that shit made me laugh. They obviously didn't know who they were fucking with.

Royal's dumb ass couldn't leave well enough alone, so he wedged his leg between old girl's, forcing her legs apart. He stuck his hand between her legs, letting his fingers slid inside her. She obviously didn't object based on the way her body reacted, but her man apparently wasn't feeling that shit. He stepped closer to the wall like he was about to lay hands on Royal, but Kay clocked his ass hard as hell.

"Bitch, didn't we just tell you she was busy?" Kay said while dude tried to regain his footing.

The next thing I know, dude jumped over the wall, followed by his two homeboys and all hell broke loose. Royal shoved old girl against the wall while he and Kay went in on her dude, and Shine and Karter took on his two homeboys. Karter was stomping the hell out of one of the dudes when I saw the other one reaching behind his back. I figured he was going for a gun, so I leaned down and rocked the shit out of him before I stood up and kicked his ass so hard in the face that two of his teeth fell out. We were beating shit out of them when the club finally caught on to what was happening, and Lincoln eventually showed up with his security.

"Yo, the fuck is going on?" he yelled, looking around. My people all looked at each other and laughed.

"Shit, these muthafuckers wanted to join our party," I said, pointing to the three dudes on the floor that we had just beat the shit out of.

"Damn King, did y'all have to fuck 'em up like that? You know I'm supposed to call the ambulance and shit," Lincoln said, looking down at them. They were clearly fucked up.

"Yo, that's on them," Royal said as he picked up a bottle of Cîroc and turned it up. Neither of us seemed bothered by what had just happened. Kay was leaning against the wall smoking a blunt, Shine had a shorty on his lap, and Karter was ordering another bottle of Hennessey from the hostess assigned to us. Lincoln's men grabbed the three dudes, helping them up.

"Get their asses out of here," Lincoln waved to the door.

"I hope this shit doesn't come back on me," Lincoln said as he massaged his temple, looking around at us.

"Man fuck them, Link. You know we got you. If they come at you playing that crying game and shit, just let me know and we'll make those bitches disappear," Royal said as he sat down, pulling dude's girl into his lap. She had obviously chosen a side, and it wasn't her man's. Old boy wore a nice ass whooping, and this bitch decided to stay and party with us. I just shook my head and laughed.

"You know we got you, Lincoln, "I said as he moved towards the entrance of VIP.

"Can we try not to have any more situations tonight," Lincoln said with smirk.

"We'll do what we can, but no promises," I said.

Lincoln just laughed and went back to entertaining the three women that were at the bar waiting on him. I took a seat on the sofa again and fired up a blunt. Hopefully the rest of our night would go smoothly.

*****

It had been a long ass night, and I was glad to be home. Being faithful while surrounded by grade-A ass just wasn't the move. I couldn't wait to be up under Free. After I got out of the shower, I wrapped a towel around my waist and went to check on Mani. It was after two, and she was fast asleep in her crib. Damn, I love this little girl more than anything.

Free was sleeping so hard that she hadn't heard me come in, and I had basically been home for an hour. I had taken a shower and turned on every light in our room, and her ass still hand budged. Now let Mani let out the slightest whimper, and I could guarantee that Free would be up in a heartbeat. That shit was crazy as hell to me, but I guess it was their connection.

Since Mani was good, I dropped my towel, locked our door, and climbed in to bed with Free. I could feel my dick getting hard just from the thought of being inside her again. When I pulled her body close to mine and realized she was naked like I requested, I swear I grew another inch.

"I missed you," Free whined when she felt my lips on her neck, and my body close to hers.

"Good, show me how much."

I grabbed her around her waist and positioned her on her back. I let my hand slide down her chest to her stomach as I smiled at her. Aside from a little pudge in her waist, you couldn't even tell she had a baby. Her breasts got a little fuller and her hips spread, but I was loving that shit. She was already sexy as fuck, but now her body was more mature.

I started a trial of kisses down her chest until I reached her center, and the second I forced her thighs apart and kissed her lips, Free grabbed my hair tight as fuck. It had been awhile since I had been between her legs, and it was clear based on her reaction.

"Damn Free, you gonna pull my fucking hair out," I said with smirk before I began to suck on her clit. She ignored me and tightened her grip on my hair, but I didn't give a fuck-I just gave her what she wanted.

"Mmmm, stop Dey," Free whined as she tried to get away from me when her orgasm started to surface, but I grabbed her waist and held on tight so that she couldn't move; within seconds, she came so hard that she damn near snapped my neck. I lifted my head and laughed and she punched me in my shoulder.

"The fuck you do that shit for?" I asked.

"Cause I told you to stop," she said.

"Man fuck that, you didn't mean that shit." I wedged myself between her legs, positioned my head at her opening, and tried to slide in, but she scooted her body away from me.

"Stop moving before I tie your little ass up," I said.

"I'm not on birth control yet. Get a condom."

I looked at Free like she was crazy. After damn near nine months of going raw, I didn't want to hear shit about a condom.

"Yes you are. I was with you when you picked that shit up today," I said, pulling her towards me again.

"No, Dey I'm not. I haven't stared it yet, and it doesn't work that fast anyway."

"You're killing my vibe, Free. I'll just pull out," I said.

"Hell no, I love Mani but I'm not going through that again anytime soon."

I was mad as hell, but I knew the only way this shit was happening right now was if I put on a condom, so I climbed out of bed, grabbed one out of the nightstand, and put that shit on.

"Now turn your ass over. Got me stressed and shit," I said.

Free just laughed and tuned over. I gently grabbed the back of her hair and entered her from the back. Her shit was tight as hell, thank God, because after watching Mani being born, a brother was worried. I sat still for a minute after I was all the way inside Free, because I felt her body tense up; I whispered against her ear.

"You good ma."

She nodded, and that was all I needed. I started working Free's body so intensely that she could barely breathe, and I didn't give a fuck. I was making up for lost time. I was hitting that shit so deep from the back that I knew I wasn't going to last long, so I made Free turn over and I let my shoulder slide under her legs, raising them in the air as I thrust inside her again. I could see everything she was feeling all over her face.

"Did you miss this?" Free nodded, but that wasn't good enough.

"Tell me," I said. "Tell me that you missed me."

"I missed you, Dey. I missed this," she said softly before she grabbed my arms and digging into my skin. Free was about to cum, and that shit was sexy as hell. I started moving faster and deeper so that we could cum together. Before long, she tightened her legs on my shoulder, and I buried my face in her neck. It was over for both of us, and we let go and let it happen. I laid there for a minute trying to get myself together because I couldn't move, and Free just looked at me and laughed.

"You alright?" she asked with a grin.

"Hell no, it's been too damn long."

"Well, you're crushing me so move," she said. I rolled over onto my back and Free snuggled close to me, resting her head on my chest.

"I love you Dey," Free said as she let her hand go up and down my chest.

"Shit I know that, how could you not?" I said just to fuck with her.

"I swear, you really know how to kill the mood."

I just laughed. "I'm just fucking with you. I love you too."

"You better," she said, and then climbed out of bed.

I watched as her sexy ass walked into the bathroom, causing me to get hard again. She just didn't know; she had a nigga caught up something terrible. I reached into the nightstand and grabbed another condom. It was time for round two. We had a lot of catching up to do.

Meka

Things between Shine and I had been weird all day, because we both knew that he was likely going to get the call today to determine whether or not Asia's baby was his. As much as I wasn't looking forward to receiving that call, I needed to know, even though I already knew. Everything in me was telling me that the baby was his and I didn't know why, but I just felt it in my gut.

I had been trying to wrap my brain around the idea of him having a child with another woman, but I just couldn't. I loved this man so much, but the thought of having to share a part of him that intimate had me damn near in tears-well, when I was infuriated and ready to take his head off for putting us in this position.

A part of me hated him for being so careless, while the rest of me loved him with my whole heart, and as insane as it was, I couldn't walk away. If I gave up on us, it was like Asia won. I knew that Shine was never going to be with Asia, not in the way that he was with me, even if I did leave. If I let her come between us, it was still like I let her win. Besides, I loved him too much to walk away. He messed up-no, he fucked up in a major way-but nobody's perfect. As long as he understood that this was his last chance, then I was going to try to make this work.

The problem was that I didn't know if I could deal with the baby. Her baby. How was I supposed to allow that baby into our home and not feel any type of way about it? I hadn't figured that part out yet, but I guess I needed to.

"What's up Meek?" Shine asked as he walked into the kitchen. I was just finishing dinner, and of course his ass was already picking at the food.

"Please wait until I fix your plate and get your nasty hands out of my pots," I smacked Shine's hand and rolled my eyes at him. Shine grabbed another steak fry and then hopped up on the island. I could feel him watching me as I moved around the kitchen.

"What?" I said dryly without looking at him, because I was getting our steaks out of the oven.

"Nothing," he said.

"Then why the hell do you keep looking at me like that," I said, now focused on him.

"You bout to fix a nigga's plate and shit," he said with a grin.

"And?"

"And that's progress," he said after he hopped down off the island, kissed me on the cheek, and then left the kitchen before I could respond. As much as I wanted to hate him, he was making it impossible.

After I had both our plates ready to go, I carried them into the living room. Shine was on the sofa with the remote in his hand, looking sexy as ever. He was in his usual fleece sweatpants with a sleeveless t-shirt on, exposing his nicely cut arms.

After I set his plate down on the table in front of him, he looked up at me and smiled before he grabbed my wrist, pulling me into his lap.

"Stanley don't," I said as I tried to get up again, but my body failed to corporate with me.

"Just chill for a minute, Meek," he said as he used his arms to hold me in place. "Look, I know you're not feeling me right now and I don't blame you. I have no right to expect you to forgive me and if you never do, there wouldn't be shit that I could say about it, but I need you to know something." He reached for my chin and turned my face so that he could see my eyes.

"I love you. Shit Meka, I have only ever loved you and I put that on everything. I might have fucked around a lot, but this shit right here is something I can't live without."

I laughed sarcastically. "I guess you should have thought about that before you decided to randomly fuck anybody that would open their legs for you." I tried to get up again, but he held on tighter.

"You're right, and I wasn't thinking about that then. I fucked up Meek and I swear on everything, if I could go back and do it all over again, I promise shit would be different, but I can't go back."

"I'm trying, Stanley. That's all I can tell you is that I'm trying."

"Do you love still love me?"

"You know I do, but just because I love you doesn't mean that I can just let it all go."

"I don't expect you to. All I want to you to do is try. Ride this shit out with me Meek, and I promise you I'll make it up to you. I'll make this shit right."

I sat there processing what he was telling me, and I wanted to give him a chance, but I knew it wasn't going to be easy. When I didn't say anything, he kept talking.

"If the baby is mine I know it's going to complicate things, but if she's mine Meek, then you know I have to be there for her. I can't have it any other way, but that doesn't mean that I expect you to be a part of her life. You don't have to, just promise me that you won't leave me."

"Let's just eat," I said; I was tired of talking about it. All I wanted was a minute where I felt like things were back the way the used to be, where it was just about us and our son.

Shine looked at me for a minute and then released his hold on me. I scooted forward and he held my waist steady to help me stand. Once I was on my feet, I handed him his plate and picked up mine before I sat down next to him. We were shoulder to shoulder, but it felt like we were miles apart. I just hoped we could figure it all out.

*****

After I ate, I decided to lay down for a while and apparently dozed off, because I woke up with Stanly next to me with his hand on my stomach. I could tell something was wrong, because he looked stressed when his eyes finally met mine.

"She's mine," he said, and then stared at me waiting for me to say something, but I didn't know what to say. I felt like I wanted to cry, but I knew that tears weren't going to change anything. Tears weren't going to change the fact that she was his.

"Okay," was all I could manage to say.

"Do you hate me?"

"I want to."

"But do you?" I didn't want to answer that, so I just changed the subject.

"Are you going to see her?" He inhaled deeply, and then let it go.

"Will you go with me?"

"I don't think that's a good idea." I didn't know if I was ready for that.

"I know that I have no right to ask you to go with me, but I don't want to do this shit by myself. You don't have to see her or be around her, but I just need you there with me."

He was frustrated and nervous. I could see it all over his face, and as much as I wanted to tell him no, I knew I couldn't do that. He needed me, and I was going to be there for him.

"Okay." Shine kissed me before he stood up and walked to the door.

"I'm about to go get dressed," he said, staring at me for a few more minutes before he walked out of our guest room. I didn't know how this was about to go, but I guess I was about to find out.

When we made it to the hospital maternity floor, Shine and I walked down the hall hand in hand. He made sure to keep me close, and I wasn't about to object. I didn't care how I felt about the situation; we were going to be a united front as far as everyone on the outside was concerned. I wasn't about to let anybody see us slipping and prey on our weakness.

As soon as we made it to Asia's room, I let go of his hand.

"I'm not going in there." I could take a lot, but seeing the three of them together wasn't something I was ready for. Shine kissed me on the cheek and then hugged me.

"I'll just get her and come out here."

I nodded, and he pushed the door open while I stood there next to it, feeling like I was about to throw up; especially after I heard Asia's voice.

"So you finally decided to act like a damn father and come see your daughter."

"Don't start with that shit. I told you I wasn't fucking with you like that until I knew for sure. Where is she anyway?" Shine sounded irritated.

"I'm fine, thanks for asking," Asia snapped.

"I don't give a fuck how you're doing. I told you this situation is strictly about my daughter. Not you."

"Hmm, that's what you're saying now, but I guarantee that will change. We're a family now, like it or not Shine."

He laughed arrogantly. "You can dead that shit, Asia. We, meaning you and me, ain't shit and never will be. The only thing we have is a daughter, so if it's not about her then you don't need to say shit to me."

"It doesn't work that way, Stanly. I call the shots as far as MY daughter is concerned, so if I say were a family then we're a family. Otherwise, you won't see her at all."

"Here's what you need to understand. That's my daughter; I got her, and she won't want for a damn thing, but I don't want or need shit from you and that will not change, are we clear?"

"Yeah, well we'll see about that," she said sarcastically. Shine let out a cocky laugh.

"Maybe I'm not being clear, so let me make sure you understand your position. I love my girl, and the idea of losing her over this shit was *enough for me to realize that I need to get it together. I will not lose her over some fuck shit, so as far as you and I are concerned, if it's not about the baby then it's not about anything, so don't come at me or my girl EVER on any bullshit on any type of level, because if you do you will come up missing, and I'll be raising her on my own. Understood?"*

"Are you threatening me?"

"Nah sweetheart, I'm not threatening you, I'm just laying out the terms of this agreement. You can either play by my rules or deal with the consequences, but either way I'm good. The choice is yours. Now I'm going to the nursery to see my daughter."

When Shine stepped out the room, he was upset; I could see it all over his face. After listening to their conversation, at least I knew where his head was at, and for now, I was okay with that.

"She's in the nursery," he said as he grabbed my hand and walked over to the nurse's station. After another thirty minutes of waiting to get him cleared to see her, I stood outside the nursery, watching as he held his daughter in his arms. He loved her, I could see it all over his face, and it had me torn. I knew that was a love I couldn't compete with while I also knew that was the same love he had for our son. My emotions were all over the place.

The ride home was quiet. There was a kind of tension around us that neither of us knew how to deal with.

"She's beautiful," I said randomly, causing Shine to glance at me for a brief moment. I could tell that he didn't know how to respond. He loved her, but he didn't want to hurt me by acknowledging it.

"Yeah she is," he finally said with a slight smile that quickly washed away when he turned to face me again.

"Don't do that," I said.

"Do what?"

"I don't ever want to be the reason why you don't show love for her. She's your daughter and I might not like the situation, but she deserves your love. She didn't ask to be here."

"Thank you. I love you Meek, and I swear on everything that I'll make this work. I promise I will."

I just smiled softly. I replayed the conversation he had with Asia in my head. I knew he loved me and I knew that he had regrets, so as long as he meant what he said then I wasn't going anywhere. We would have to figure this out. It wasn't going to be easy, but love is complicated. *Right?*

Karter

I looked around the warehouse office while we waited for Del to show up. This would be the first time that Kay and I met him since partnering with King, Royal, and Shine. My mind was a million places except here. I had spent that last week following my next target, while trying to make sure Mo was good. She seemed to be doing fine, but I could still occasionally see a sadness in her eyes that made my blood boil. I tried not to let it get to me too much, and just surrounded her with as much love that I could give her. It was all I could do to make things right.

"What's on your mind, Karter?" Kay asked after he sat down next to me. I looked up, and Royal was on the phone with who I assumed was Lace, based on the way his bipolar ass was talking. King and Shine were deep in conversation about King wanting a new bike.

"Just business," I said as I let my head fall back, closing my eyes. I was tired as hell and hadn't really been sleeping because of the time I spent on my current target, but it was worth a lot of money so I didn't really mind.

"You on a job?" Kay asked. I opened my eyes briefly to find him watching me before I closed them again.

"Yeah what's up?"

"Your ass needs to take a break. You barely sleep as it is. How's Mo anyway?"

I chuckled. "Is this about me not sleeping or about Mo?"

"Both muthafucker. So how is she?" I could hear the smile in my brother's voice. He was worried about me, but he was also concerned about Mo.

"She's good. She's at the house with Sasha right now, so you know how that shit goes. Sasha is loving it. Mo has my baby girl thinking she's a model and shit."

I couldn't help but smile when I thought about the two of them together. Mo was more of a mother to Sasha than Saria's trifling ass had ever been, and that had me wanting to make Saria disappear.

Kay laughed. "You better hope Mo has a boy or you're gonna be fucked."

"Shit I know, but it's all good."

The alarm caught all of our attention when it went off, letting us know that someone was on the property, so I opened my eyes and sat up.

"That's Del," King said after looking at the laptop to check the security monitor.

"Aight, let's do this shit, I have to get my ass home and do some quality control. Lace is trying to turn my house into a Barbie mansion. Her ass has got pink and purple shit everywhere. I'm about to dead that."

"Your dumb ass is the one that forced her to move in, so don't get mad about the fact that she wants to make her house too," Shine said, looking at Royal like he was crazy

"Shit, fuck that. It is her house, but that don't mean I want purple curtains, pillows, and shit like that everywhere. The fuck I look like?"

"Lace is gonna fuck you up, and when she does I'll be there like I told your dumb ass," Shine said as we all left the office.

This was my first time laying eyes on Delgado, and he looked just like I imaged. Dressed in an all-black overpriced custom-made suit with caramel skin and black and grey hair slicked back. He had a neatly trimmed goatee and you couldn't really see his age on him, other than the grey that was filtered through out his head.

"King, Royal, Shine. It's good to see you again," he spoke in a think Spanish accent as he extended a hand to each of them, one by one, before pulling them into a hug. Del turned to face Kay and I, and after he checked us out, he spoke again.

"You must be Karter and Kay?"

He extended a hand to Kay and I, going through the same process that he down with King, Royal, and Shine. He surveyed our faces for a minute silently before he turned to King.

"So they're family?"

"Yeah."

"Well good. I see no issues with that," Del said, offering a smile as he looked around at all of us.

"They had their own territory that they brought in, on top of the fact that we're selling shit like crazy, so that's why our order is so big," King glanced at all of us.

"No problem, King. Your money is good with me. You buy, I'll sell."

"Well, let's get this taken care of. I know you guys have more important things to do than to entertain an old man like myself," Del said with a smirk.

We all followed him outside, and his men opened the rear of the two Range Rovers that were behind Del's Benz.

Royal and Kay checked the product while King, Shine, and I got Del's money out the back of King's truck. After everyone was satisfied, we all said our goodbyes. King made it clear to Del that Kay and I were equal partners, which meant that it was possible that in the future Kay and I might be there to handle shipments alone. Del agreed and was on his way.

"Call La and tell her to get packaging out here so that we can get this shit ready to hit the streets," King said to Shine.

"Already on it," he said as he pulled his phone out.

"How's Mo?" King asked after he approached me, folding his arms.

"She's good."

"That's good to hear. Shit like that will fuck with you. When it happened to Free, it took me a minute to let that shit go, and still to this day I think about, it but you can't let it control you."

"I'm straight, and I appreciate you and the team being there."

"We're family. That's what we do." King extended his hand to me, which I accepted, and then he pulled me into a brief hug before he nodded and walked off.

After we got the product situated, I climbed in my Porsche and headed home, stuck in my thoughts. I planned on taking out my target tonight, but right now I was going home to spend time with Mo and Sasha. The second I hit the highway, my phone went off, so I hit Bluetooth without checking to see who was calling.

"Yeah."

"Where are you?" Saria's annoying ass yelled.

"What do want, Saria?"

"I want to know where my daughter is. You better not have her around that bitch." I tightened my grip on the steering wheel, trying to calm myself.

"What did I tell you about that shit, Saria? Call Mo something other than her name one more time, and I'm fucking you up."

"Whatever Karter. You're acting all brand new since you have her now. Does she know that you're still fucking me?" I laughed because Saria was putting on a show, hoping that Mo was around me to hear the conversation. I hadn't been with Saria in months, and she knew it.

"No she doesn't know, because we both know that shit is a lie. Just because you dream about my dick every night doesn't mean I had my shit in you, so kill that stupidity you're talking."

"Fuck you Karter, we both know you're coming back. You always do," she yelled. I laughed, because her little feelings were hurt.

"You sucking my dick is not me coming back. It's you giving a brother head, simple as that but trust me, that shit's over too. I'm good on that; all my needs are being met."

"Kiss my ass Karter, and tell that bitch to watch her back. She'll never see me coming," Saria said, and hung up the phone.

I jumped off the exit and redirected myself towards Saria's house. She had just crossed the line, and apparently I needed to pay her a visit to teach her dumb ass a lesson. When I pulled up at her house, I was fuming. The grass wasn't cut, the trashcan was sitting in front of the garage over flowing, and she had Sasha's toys thrown all across the yard.

I used my key to get in and almost lost it. The damn place smelled foul as shit. I followed the smell to the kitchen and the sink was full of dishes, the counters were covered with take out, and there were several bags of trash piled up next to the pantry.

Feeling like I was about to take a life, I made my way to the master bedroom and pushed the door open. Saria's stupid ass was sitting on the edge of the bed smoking a blunt, with a bottle of vodka on the floor in front of her. I walked up to her and smacked the shit out of her, causing her to fall back before I grabbed her by the neck and pulled her off the bed, dragging her towards the kitchen.

"Is this how you have my daughter living!" I yelled as I pushed her ass to the floor of her nasty ass kitchen.

Saria looked up at me with fear in her eyes. She knew I didn't play this shit. I bought her this nice ass house to make sure my daughter was living well, and she had my shit looking like the fucking projects. Hell, if her lazy ass wasn't going to clean it herself, the least she could do was hire somebody to do it for her. She knew I would pay for that shit.

I knew she was lazy as fuck but at least she used to try, but I guess since I wasn't coming around anymore she was like fuck it. I wondered why her ass was always so damn eager to meet me somewhere when I was getting Sasha.

"I'm sorry Karter," she cried after she was on her feet and backing away from me, making sure she that she was out of my reach.

"You damn right you are. This shit don't make any sense. How the fuck you live in this nice ass house but got this shit looking like a damn overpriced crack house?"

She looked around as embarrassment filled her face. "It's not always like this. I just didn't feel like cleaning up this morning," she said trying to explain.

"Oh, so you think I'm fucking stupid. This shit is more than just one day. No wonder why Sasha hates being here with your ass. She cries every time she knows that she's going home, but you don't have to worry about that shit anymore. My daughter will not be living in this type of environment."

"You're not taking my daughter, Karter!" Saria rushed me swinging, but I shoved her ass back, causing her to hit the floor again.

I just looked at her pathetic ass as she tried to stand again, but I turned to leave instead of entertaining her bullshit. She was right behind me yelling like she had lost her mind.

"You're not about to let that bitch play mommy to my daughter. She's mine, Karter. I'll send your ass to jail before I let that happen."

Hearing her say that made me snap. I felt my body go cold, and I zoned out. I turned around, back handed Saria, and she went flying across the room. With three long strides, I had her around the neck again as I pulled my gun out of my jeans and pointed it at her head.

"What the fuck did you just say?" I yelled through clenched teeth.

"Nothing...I.....I....didn't say anything," she stuttered as the reality of her mistake began to settle in. Kay wasn't here to save her dumb ass this time. I tighten my grip on her neck as tear fell from her eyes.

"You're a dumb bitch. All you have to do is play your role and take care of my daughter. I give you everything you want, and all I ask is that you be a good fucking mother, but no you can't do that shit. You got your ass in the fucking strip club and living like a fucking crack whore. Do you want to die?"

She looked at me with a fear that I knew too well. I had seen it thousands of times before in my targets when they knew I was about to take their lives.

"Open your fucking mouth, do you want to die?"

"No," she mumbled.

"Then don't ever threaten me like that again. Are we understood?"

"Yes."

I leaned in and kissed her gently on the lips. "Good, now clean this fucking house up. Consider me Social Services. You just lost custody of your daughter until I feel like you can handle the responsibility of raising her. I'll be stopping by randomly to make sure you're living right but as for Sasha, she's staying with me."   I let her go and started walking to the front door.

"Karter, please don't take my baby. I promise I'll do what I'm supposed to. Just don't take Sasha, Karter, please."

"Man, save that shit. You should have thought about that a long time ago. Get your shit together Saria, and maybe I'll let you see her, but she's not staying in this house anymore."

I walked out and left her there in tears. I didn't give a fuck. I gave her too many chances to get her shit together and she just wouldn't listen, so I had no emotions about it.

After I made it to my apartment, I sat in the car for a minute to get my head right. Saria had me mad as fuck, and I didn't want to take it out on Mo. When I was finally ready, I got out and made my way into the elevator. The second the doors opened, I saw Mo and my baby girl sitting on the floor going through one of Mo's jewelry boxes. Sasha saw me jumped up and ran into my arms.

"Daddy look," she said, holding out her tiny little hand to show me her pink nails. I scooped her up into my arms and walked over to the sofa to sit down with her in my lap.

"I see. Very pretty," I winked at her before I pecked her on the lips.

"Mo did it and my, toes too," she said, extending her legs so that I could see her matching pink toenails.

"I don't think you're old enough for all that," I said with a playful scowl.

"Yes I am, I'm five," she said confidently with a frown before she wiggled her way out of my lap and returned to the floor in front of Mo's jewelry box.

Mo stood up and let her hand run down Sasha's arm before she walked over and sat down beside me, looping her arm through mine.

"How did it go?" she asked as she looked up at me.

"It was straight," I leaned down and kissed her.

"Are you done for the day?"

"Until tonight, what's up?"

"I was thinking maybe we could go out for a while. Lane called and asked if we wanted to do lunch with her and Kay. I was thinking that would be nice."

She laid her head on my shoulder. "Yeah we can do that." I was just happy to see her smiling.

"I'm about to get dressed then." She pulled away slightly to get up, but I stopped her.

"I need to talk to you about something," I glanced at Sasha and then looked back at Mo.

"Is something wrong?" she gave me a concerned stare.

"Nah, I just need for Sasha to stay here with us for a while," I said, and then waited for her to respond.   A smile grew across her face as she looked over at Sasha.

"She's your daughter, Karter. I would never have a problem with that. I know what she means to you and besides, I could use a little more diva around here. She mellows you out anyway," Mo said with a grin.

"Are you sure?" I asked

"I love you and I love her. Sasha being here is understood, no matter what the arrangements are."

"Thank you." Mo playfully punched me in the shoulder before she got up and walked over to Sasha.

"Come on lady bug, let's get dressed so we can go see Uncle Kay and Lane."

Sasha jumped up smiling, placed her tiny little hand in Mo's, and my two girls disappeared into the bedroom. The both had my heart, there wasn't any question about that.

Kay

"Laney, are you ready?" I yelled over my shoulder as I sat on the sofa flipping through channels impatiently.

I had been sitting in my living room waiting on Lane for the past twenty minutes, after she told me an hour ago that she was *almost* ready. I was quickly learning that I needed to take almost as two hours, and then I might be able to nail down an exact departure time.

"Here I come!" she yelled back, and a few minutes later she appeared, making me smile as my eyes searched her body.

She was wearing a leather fedora with her thick, curly hair hanging out the back, tan skinny jeans, and a brown cashmere sweater that matched her hat. Damn, she was sexy as hell.

"You look good as fuck Laney, but did it really take all that?" I stood up and approached her, locking my arms behind her back as I kissed her deeply.

"You're so impatient," she said as soon as we released our kiss.

I laughed. "And for good reason, you take forever."

"Perfection takes time," she said, and then adjusted her oversized purse on her shoulder.

165

"You're perfect without even trying." I moved towards the door, holding it open as I waited for her to walk through it.

After I locked the door and we were in my Charger, she looked at me and with a grin. "You're just saying that because you want me to get ready faster."

"I'm saying it because it's true," I paused, "and because I want you to get ready faster." She rolled her eyes at me and pulled out her phone.

"Have you talked to your mom lately?"

"Yeah why?"

"No reason, I was just thinking maybe we could go see here soon," Lane said and then looked at me, trying to gauge my reaction

"We can do that, but what's up?"

"Nothing, she just asked me to make sure I came to visit, and I promised I would and I haven't seen her since."

I couldn't control my smile. "Oh, so now you want to be friends with Sheila. Before you were all *I'm going to kill you, Kay.*"

"That's because you didn't give me a choice. You just sent me off to meet her by myself with no warning or anything." Lane looked at me and frowned, making me laugh.

"It's cool, I'll set something up."

Just because I hated Liam's bitch ass didn't mean that I didn't love my mother. We talked all the time, but I hadn't really seen her much because I refused to go to the house. I didn't want to run the risk of having to deal with my father, but if Lane wanted to spend time with my mother, then I was going to make that happen.

We arrived at the restaurant about twenty minutes later, and I parked and opened Lane's door, waiting for her to get out. As soon as we were inside, Sasha spotted us; I heard her yell my name and come running in my direction.

"Uncle K, what took you so long? We've been here forever," she said as I scooped her up and started kissing her little face.

"Forever? I don't think you've been here forever, lady bug."

"We have, ask daddy," she grinned and pointed to their booth.

"Well I'm glad you didn't leave, because I would have missed you too much." I held her in place with one arm while I placed my other hand on Lane's back as we went to join Karter and Mo.

Mo stood up to hug Lane while Karter and I dapped each other before everyone took their seats. Sasha sat in between Karter and Mo on one side of the booth, while Lane and I sat across from them on the other side.

167

"Look!" Sasha yelled as she held her hand out towards Lane, who reached across the table and took Sasha's tiny hand into hers to examine her pink nails.

"Wow, I like it. Who did that, pretty girl?" Lane asked. Sasha leaned into Mo's side, grinning. "Mo did it. She did my hair too. Daddy can only do one ponytail," she looked up at Karter and frowned.

"It's like that, baby girl?" Karter asked, and then laughed.

With one look at Sasha's hair, we all new Karter had no parts in it. She had some long braid circling her head and ending in wild puff on the side. I swear, if I ever had a daughter she would be screwed if I have to be responsible for her head. Sasha had long, thick curly hair that reached her shoulders.

"It's true, Daddy. You always do one ponytail," Sasha giggled before she picked up her crayons and started coloring on her kids menu.

"You look good, Mo," I said, checking her out. She was always flawless, which I assumed was mostly out of habit because she had modeled basically her whole life. She once showed me a print ad she had done for Gap when she was five.

She smiled softly. "Thanks Kay. I'm happy." She looked across at Karter and smiled. She was good for him, and I was glad that he was finally settling down.

"How's the pregnancy going?" Lane asked, causing Mo to light up even more.

"So far so good. I think I'm finally over the morning sickness."

"She still don't eat shit, though," Karter said with a little too much aggression, leading me to believe that must have been a sore subject with them.

"I eat, just not as much as you do," Mo said.

"Daddy look," Sasha said, holding up her menu to show Karter where she had written her name.

"Very good," Karter said as he leaned down to kiss Sasha. "You're super smart."

"Just like you, Daddy."

"Nah, just like me," I said and winked at Sasha, who smiled.

"So how does that work with modeling, being pregnant and all?" Lane asked.

"They're cool with it. I actually have a few shoots set up for a maternity line," Mo said as she glanced at Karter. I knew my brother, and I knew he was having no parts of Mo being on the road traveling while she was carrying his child.

"How does that work after you have the baby?" Lane asked.

"I haven't really thought about that yet," Mo said.

"It doesn't work," Karter said, causing Mo to look uncomfortable.

"What about you two? It's about time for your first one," Mo smiled at lane.

"Yeah Laney, what about us?" I asked, placing my arm around her shoulders and pulling her into my side.

"What about us?" Lane said, rolling her eyes at me.

"Karter's working on his second; can I at least get my first?" I said with a smirk.

"You are not ready for a baby, Kayman," Lane said firmly.

"Shit, fuck that. He's more ready than I am, and I already have one," Karter said, and then laughed.

"I guess you heard that," I said.

"We'll talk about that another time," Lane said.

"Yeah, when we get home right before I bust that nut up in you," I said, and then kissed her on the neck.

"Kayman." Lane looked down at Sasha, who was not paying us any attention. She was biting down on her bottom lip, going in on a dot-to-dot activity that was on her kids menu.

Mo and Karter both laughed at me. "I guess you heard that, Laney," Karter said, mocking my nickname for Lane.

"I'm not worried about Kayman and he knows that," Lane said.

"Maybe not right now, but you will be in about," I held my arm up and looked at the watch on my wrist. "In about another hour, two tops."

Lane nailed me in my shoulder with her bony fist, and then picked up her menu. She could play all she wanted to but, her little ass was about to be pregnant by the end of the month.

After we ordered and our food arrived, we ate and talked for a while and then left the restaurant. I had to promise Sasha a trip to Fly Zone because she wanted to go with me, but I had plans to make a baby with Lane, so it would have to wait. The girls got in the cars, and I stood outside to talk to my brother for a minute.

"You talk to Mom?"

"Nah not today, what's up?'

"Nothing, Lane asked about seeing her so I was thinking about maybe having dinner or something with her and Ky. You down?"

"Yeah that's cool. Just let me know when."

"I will. So what's up with you and Mo?"

"What do you mean?"

"You knew who she was before you got her pregnant. You can't expect her to just let that shit go."

"Man, fuck that. She's not about to be flying around the country while she's carrying my damn baby." Just mentioning it had Karter pissed off.

"I agree but, you need to figure out what's next. You can't make her leave the only life she's ever known. That shit won't work, and you know it. She'll resent you. You'll be mad at her, and that shit will fall apart. I know you love her, so you have to figure something out."

"What the fuck ever. She just needs to accept the fact that she's about to be a mother."

"Did you hear anything I just said? That's like her telling you that you had to get out the game or some bullshit like that. What if she didn't want you doing any more hits?"

"That's different."

"How muthafucker? You being a hired gun is way more dangerous than her doing a fucking photo shoot. What's the worst that could happen, a damn wardrobe malfunction or some shit like that? But your ass could catch a fucking bullet doing what you do."

Karter looked at me for a second before he laughed. "You're dumb as fuck, you know that?"

"Fuck you Karter, I'm serious," I said through a laugh.

"I hear you. We'll figure that shit out," Karter said.

"You better, shit I actually like Mo, and if y'all don't make it you'll be alone like a muthafucker, because I'll be hating like a bitch on any other shorty's you try to hook up with."

"Damn Kay, that's fucked up. You're always supposed to be on my side," Karter said, mugging me hard as hell.

"I am, that's why I'm trying to make sure you get shit right with Mo."

"I feel you," Karter said. He extended a fist to me, and I met it with mine before we went our separate ways. I loved my brother, but he didn't always think logically when it came to the people he loved. It was his way of keeping them safe, but sometimes he couldn't see past that in order to make sure they were also happy.

*****

"What are you doing in here?" Lane walked into my office and sat down next to me on my sofa.

"Just going over my accounts," I said, and then closed my laptop and sat it on the floor in front of me before pulling Lane across my lap. "What's up, what's on your mind?"

"Nothing, I was just wondering what you were up to."

"You miss me Laney?" I kissed her on the neck, and then started gently biting down on it.

"I always miss you when you're not close to me," she said.

"Oh yeah?" I asked with raised eyebrows.

Lane turned her body so that she was straddling me, and then placed her arms around my neck.

"Yeah." She leaned in to kiss me, so I let my hands slid up her back and then down to her ass.

"You know I was serious, right?" I asked, looking her right in the eyes.

She stared back at me confused. "About what?"

"I want a baby Laney."

"Kayman--"

"What, Lane? Don't tell me that I don't know what I want, because I know what I fucking want. This shit right here is permanent. It's just you and me, so I'm not going anywhere and I want a baby, with you and only you."

"What if I don't want a kid? I don't know what to do with a kid. My mother loved me, but she spent most of her time chasing Wesley and the only love Wesley ever showed me was signing a check, so how am I supposed to love a baby?"

The seriousness in her voice let me know that she was struggling with the idea. I guess I never really thought about it. Liam might not have been the best father, but growing up he always showed us love and when he didn't, my mother loved Karter and I enough for the both of them, so I never struggled with that; it was just natural.

I pulled Lane into my chest and locked my arms around her body. "You will love our baby the way that you love me. That's all that you have to do, Laney."

We sat there without words, her head resting on my shoulder and my arms securely around her body. Our breathing fell in sync, and it was like we became one. I loved her more than anything and I knew she loved me just as much, so we would figure it out. We had to.

King

"Damn Free, she's fat as hell, what the fuck you feeding her?" Royal asked as he held Imani on his lap.

"What did I tell you about cussing around my baby, Royal? And she's not fat."

"Shit, yes hell she is," he said, and then busted out laughing, making Free walk over to him and slap him upside the head.

I watched as Royal's dumb ass sat there making faces at Mani, trying to get her to laugh. She was three months old now, and she was definitely a little chunk. Her greedy ass didn't miss any meals, but I loved my baby girl so she was perfect.

"You love the way Uncle Royal talks, don't you Mani-Mani," Royal said, sounding retarded trying to do baby talk, but Imani went crazy smiling and making noise, so Royal looked up at Free.

"See, she loves the way I talk, Free. Mani-Mani, tell your mommy to stop trying to change Uncle Royal and love me for me," he said and then mugged Free, who was walking out of the living room shaking her head.

"Aight, keep bouncing her like that and her little ass is gonna throw up on you. You know she's good for that."

"Nah, she knows what's up. Isn't that right, Mani-Mani?" Royal kissed her chubby cheeks, and again she want wild, up until Mira walked up and snatched her off Royal's lap.

"Why you take her Mira?" Royal asked, eyeing my sister.

"Because she loves me more, and we've got some girl talk to do," Mira said, sticking her tongue out at Royal.

"Aight, you remember that shit the next time King won't let your ass do something and you call me crying about it."

"I will, because you'll still take my side anyway," Mira said over her shoulder as she left the room with Mani in her arms. Royal just shook his head and laughed, because he knew she was right. He was good cop and I was bad cop when it came to Mira, and it had always been that way.

"Yo, you ready to hit the lot?" Royal asked.

"Yeah, let me get my keys."

We were both thinking about selling our bikes and getting new ones, so we were about to hit up the dealership to figure out what we wanted to buy.

"What lot?" Free asked as she walked up behind me and wrapped her arms around my waist.

"We're going to check out some new bikes so I can decide what I want," I said.

"I want to go?" she said, looking up at me.

"The fuck you wanna go for? You don't ride?" Royal said.

"Only because I couldn't. Don't forget his sneaky ass got me pregnant as soon as we met, so I've literally been pregnant almost the entire time we've been together."

"So you wanna ride?" I asked, pulling Free from behind me. The idea of her on a bike was making me shit swell a little.

"Yeah, take me."

"Aight, let's go. I'll take you real quick and if you like it, then you can go with us and I'll get you your own bike."

"Seriously?'

"Yeah, if you want one I'll get you one."

"You can't put a damn baby on a bike, Free," Royal said with a grin.

"I know that, dumb ass. Mira can watch her. I'll be right back." She took off up the stairs, leaving us.

"You really want her on a bike?"

"He'll yeah, that shit is sexy as fuck." Royal's dumb ass let a smile cross his face.

"You're right. I might get Lace one too but, she'll have to get a moped or some shit like that, cause she short as fuck," he said, making both of us laugh.

"I'm telling her you said that," Free said, rolling her eyes at Royal.

"Damn Free, can a brother have any secrets?"

"Not when you're talking about my girl."

Free sat on the sofa and pulled on some bright, over-the-top colorful ass Nikes and, then pulled an equally bright sweatshirt over her head. She was already in a pair of grey leggings, looking sexy as hell.

"I'm ready," she said, grinning like a little kid.

"Aight, let's go." we walked through the kitchen to the garage, and I got an extra helmet for my bike and handed it to Free before; I then let the door up and backed my bike out. When I had it in the driveway, she climbed on and pulled the helmet down over her head.

"Wrap your arms around my waist and hold on tight."

"Don't let me fall off, Dey."

"Just hold on, I got you."

Royal was already on his bike and when I waved my hand, he took off in front of us. Free had her arms securely around my waist, and I could feel her head on my back as we took off, heading towards the gate. A few minutes later, we were on the road. Royal's reckless ass was driving like a

179

maniac, but I started off slow, giving Free a minute to get used to it before I finally gave in and caught up with him.

I loved having Free on my bike with me. That shit had me hyped. Hell, Free might not be getting her own shit. She could just ride with me.

Thirty minutes later, we were at the dealership and we pulled up and parked. Free got off and pulled her helmet from her head, looking happy as hell.

"I want my own," she said.

I climbed off my bike and placed my helmet on the handle. "Nah, I changed my mind. I want you riding with me," I said, causing her to frown at me.

"You said if I liked it I could get my own."

"I'm just playing, come on."

We spent the next hour trying out bikes and before I left, I had two custom bikes-one for me, and one for Free. I'd also spent way more than I had planned. That shit didn't matter though, because I had it to spend. Free's spoiled ass went home pouting because she didn't realize that she had to have a separate license to ride her bike, so we were calling next week to get her set up to take lessons and get her permit.

We were finally home, and Free was sitting in the center of the floor in the living room Indian style with Imani in her lap. I was on the sofa with the TV on, but watching the two of them.

"Why are you looking at me like that?" Free looked up at me and smiled.

"You're just different now," I said honestly, and hell she was. Next month will be a year since we met, and thinking back to the person she was back then to who she had become now made me smile.

"Different how?" she asked. It made me laugh thinking about it.

"Well for starters, I just bought you a customized bike, you carry a gun, you cuss my ass out on the regular, bossing up on me if I even think about doing some foul shit, so you're a lot different now."

She looked at me with a smirk. "It's your fault. You corrupted me."

"He sure did. I don't even recognize you anymore," Mira said when she walked into the living room and laid down on the floor, pulling Mani out of Free's lap.

"Nah, I just helped the real you come out. You can only be who you really are," I said.

Free laughed. "So I was always secretly a street king's queen and I just didn't know it."

"Hell yeah. I knew from day one that you would be down. It was just gonna take some time to get you right. I had to deprogram all that high class private school shit."

"Really, cause I distinctly remember you telling me more than once that I wasn't cut out for this lifestyle, and that I needed to get it together if we were gonna make it," Free said, narrowing her eyes at me.

I smiled. "It was all a plan, kind of like that Scared Straight shit they do on TV, where they take those bad ass kids to jail to let them see how their lives will turn out if they didn't get their shit together. Me telling you that was like those kids being in jail."

"Shut up Dey, you're so stupid." Free threw one of Mani's stuffed animals at me.

"It don't matter how it happened. You're my little rider, and that's what's up. Especially now that I know you'll body a nigga for me."

"Only when necessary," Free said.

"Alright Bonnie and Clyde," Mira said, rolling her eyes at both of us.

If anybody had asked me a year ago if this would be my life I damn sure never would have agreed, but now that I'm living it I couldn't see it any other way.

*****

The sound of my phone going off woke me up, so I reached over and grabbed it, seeing an unlisted number.

"Yeah," I answered, a little annoyed.

"Dey, were you sleeping?"

I immediately sat up. "Yeah but it's cool Pops, you good? Everything alright." I knew my pops had privilege in prison, so I wasn't surprised to get a call from him, but the timing had me concerned.

"Shit is lovely. Couldn't be better other than the fact that I need a ride."

I held my phone away from my face briefly and then back to my ear, thinking that I must be losing it. I know he didn't just say he needed a ride.

"You need a ride?" I asked confused.

"You heard me correct. I'm officially a free man. So how about you head down here and come get me," my father said, sounding happy as hell. I knew my father and he wasn't really the joking type; in fact, he was typically always about business, so to hear him say that he was a free man had me shocked as hell.

"Free, how?"

"I'll explain when you get here. Just hurry up. I'm ready to see my baby girl and hold my granddaughter.

"You're fucking with me, right?" I asked, stilling needing clarification and now Free was up staring at me trying to figure out what was going on.

"Dey, come and get me. We'll talk when you get here," my dad said firmly.

183

"I'm on my way," I said, and then ended the call.

"Who was that?" Free asked as I climbed out of bed.

"My father."

I stood there for a minute with my arms folded, processing what had just happened. My pops was serving a life sentence for shooting Shy right in front of a cop, so I didn't see how there was any way that he should be free. He was not eligible for parole, so I was extremely confused, but fuck it. My pops was coming home and I was happy as hell. I didn't give a fuck how it happened; I was just glad it happened.

"What's wrong, is he okay?"

"Apparently he's more than okay. He called to ask me to come and get him. He's free."

"Wait, I thought he had a life sentence, how?"

"I don't know. He said he would explain when I got there. I don't really give a fuck. I'm just going to get him."

Free looked at me and smiled. "I'm happy for you. I can't wait to meet him."

My pops and Free talked on the phone, but he never wanted her to come there to see him. It was kind of the same reasoning he had with keeping Mira away. He didn't want to put them at risk by being associated with him. My pops still had a lot of enemies, and being in prison didn't erase that.

I walked into the closet and threw on a pair of sweats. I couldn't believe that my pops was officially a free man again. That shit had a nigga in his feelings something serious. It was like I was that sixteen-year-old kid again who had to watch my pops handcuffed, being escorted out of the courtroom after the judge had given him life with no parole. I was happy as hell, and I knew that Mira was going to lose it the second she laid eyes on him.

"I'm out." I kissed Free, grabbed my phone, keys, and walked out of our bedroom door.

"Be careful, Dey."

"Always, you already know," I said, and then shut our door.

It was two o'clock in the morning, so I decided not to wake Mira; besides, I wanted to surprise her. I knew she was going to lose it. She missed our father so much. She was always a daddy's girl, and when he got locked up it killed her. I had to take over for her and even though she loved me, I knew it wasn't the same as having my pops there for her. That was part of the reason why I spoiled her so much. It was my way of trying to make up for the fact that our pops was gone.

I stopped by Mani's room, and of course my little chunk was sleeping peacefully. I kissed her chubby cheeks and then headed downstairs. I made my way through the garage and climbed in my G Wagon.

It was an hour's drive to the prison, but today that shit didn't even faze me because hopefully it was the last trip I would ever have to make there. I was bringing my pops home.

AK

Dirty cops are a criminal's best friend. My lawyer had finally got my case thrown out, and as much as they hated it they couldn't do shit about it. I was lucky enough that the cop that I shot Shy in front of was dirty as fuck, along with his partner. On top of that, they were working with a dirty District Attorney, so almost every case they had their hands in was overturned. The city was mad as hell, but oh well; shit happens.

Wesley's bitch ass was trying his best to keep me locked up, but all this shit happened before he was district attorney, so his hands were tied. The city was trying to avoid lawsuits, so as of now, there were a lot of free muthafuckers who probably should have been up under the jail-myself included.

Now, all in needed to complete this situation was to put a bullet in Wesley. His bitch ass had been creating problems for my son and Free, and then he also tried to keep me locked up. He was gonna have to pay for that with his life. Dey might have promised Free that he wouldn't touch Wesley but fuck it, I never did. Wesley was going to die and real soon2405266264 and then I was done. After that, I had to live by the law because there was no way I was going back to prison.

"Kingston, your ride is here." I stood up and smiled as all eyes were on me. A few of the guards were happy for me while most of them didn't hide the fact that they couldn't believe that I was about to walk out of there. I smiled as I made my way through the door with nothing but the clothes on my back that I came in with. That shit didn't faze me, because I had a small fortune waiting on me on the outside.

When I laid eyes on my son and there wasn't a glass wall or a table in between us, I felt tears forming. I had missed so much of his life and I couldn't get that back, but believe me when I say that I was going to appreciate every second of every minute that we had together from here on out

As soon as I was face to face with my son, I pulled him into my chest and hugged him so tightly that my arms were tired when I finally released him. Even though I saw him for an occasional visit, it was clear that he had changed. He still had that wild curly hair, but he no longer had the face of a boy. My son was now a man with a family of his own, and I respected him for that. He had raised my daughter and was now raising his own.

"You look good old man," Dey said as we made our way to his ride, G Wagon; typical Diego. Nice as hell, but not so much that it threw up red flags. I guess I taught him well.

"Watch that old man shit, Dey." I couldn't help but smile as I sat next to my son and we pulled off, en route to his house.

"I'll chill with the old man shit if you chill with all that staring like you're looking at a fucking ghost."

I laughed. "Not a ghost, son. Just a stranger. I hardly recognize you anymore, but that's a good thing. You're a man now."

Diego smiled and nodded, "You're damn straight, but I'm still your son pops."

"How's Mira? Does she know yet?"

"Nah, her little ass would have been right here with me. I decided to wait and let you surprise her."

"Aight cool. I miss my baby girl. Well I guess she not really a baby any more, is she?"

Dey glanced at me, and I could tell from the way he was looking at me that he could feel my sadness. Not only had I missed out on his life, but I missed hers too.

"She's still a damn baby. Spoiled as ever too. Not much has changed with that. She just grew a little bit," Diego laughed a little, likely thinking about his sister.

"I hope not. I miss her like crazy and I know she didn't really understand my reasons for keeping her away, but it was for her own good."

"Nah, she's good. She gets it. She wasn't happy about it, but she eventually understood."

We drove in silence for a while before he finally questioned me about my freedom.

"So, what's the deal pops? How did this happen?"

"Long story short, the cops and DA that handled my case were dirty as fuck. Griffin has been working on getting my case thrown out for a while now, but it was tricky because I killed Shy in front of a bunch of witnesses. Shit finally fell into place, and here I am. They can't try me again for the same case, so I'm a free man and plan on staying that way."

I looked at Dey and I couldn't read his mood, but he didn't seem happy.

"So Griffin's been working on this for a while, huh?"

"Yeah why?" I asked, already knowing the answer.

"Then why the fuck didn't I know about it? I might have been able to help get you out sooner," he said with venom dripping from his voice while he tried to remain respectful.

"I didn't want to tell you and then shit didn't work out. There was no point involving you in it. I had it under control."

"Yeah, I guess so."

"Look Diego, the day they escorted me out of the courtroom was the worst day of my life. The look on your face, your mother's face, broke me. I never in my life felt like less of a man. I knew I let you guys down, and there wasn't anything that I could do about it. I refused to see that look on your face again, so maybe I should have told you but I didn't. I needed to do this on my own so that if shit didn't work out, you would never have known that there was even a possibility of me being free again. Do you understand that?" I waited as my son took time to process what I said, and the he finally spoke.

"I get it. I probably would have done the same thing but fuck it, you're here now and that's all that matters."

*****

I woke up the next morning, or rather a few hours later, in the guestroom of my son's house, feeling like a new man. It was just after six; I guess old habits die hard. I was used to being up early, so I figured that it was going to be almost impossible for me to sleep late.

I climbed out of bed and dressed in the sweats that my son had given me before I left my room heading downstairs. Once I made it to the kitchen, I walked in and startled Free, who had my granddaughter in her arms while she struggled to make her a body. I couldn't help but smile.

"Sorry, I didn't mean to scare you," I said as I walked in and stood beside her, admiring the beauty she was holding in her arms.

"It's fine. I'm usually the only one up this early," she said with a smile.

"Yeah, I guess it is kind of early."

"Do you wanna hold her?" Free asked when she noticed my focus was on the baby.

"Yeah I do."

I reached for her, and the second I had her in my arms her tiny little fist went right for my face. She was the most beautiful thing I had ever laid my eyes on with her big round eyes and fat chubby cheeks. She had a head full of hair that was wild and all over her head, making her look just like Diego, so I kind of laughed.

"What?" Free asked, smiling at the two of us.

I ran my hand across her hair. "She looks just like Dey."

Free grinned. "I know, it's not as bad when I braid it or put in in ponytails, but she just got up. Dey hates when I do anything too it. I think he likes it all over her head because he knows it makes them look alike."

"I can understand that. He loves this little girl," I said as I kissed her chubby cheeks.

"Yes he does," Free said as she turned to face me now that she had the bottle ready.

"Come on, you can feed her," Free said leaving the kitchen, so I followed and got comfortable on the sofa, with Free on the love seat across from me.

"It's been a longtime since I've done this," I looked up at Free and smiled. She was a beautiful woman, and I could see why my son was so in love with her. I was just glad that he was happy.

"I can't tell. She seems content." I looked down as my granddaughter went to town on her bottle.

"How did you sleep?"

"Best few hours of sleep I've had in a long time," I chuckled.

"Well I'm glad. I'm happy you're here. They miss you so much," Free said sincerely, which made me think about the fact that she no longer had a connection with her father.

"I've missed them too."

"Have you talk to Mira yet?"

"Not yet. I was going to wait until she wakes up."

"I don't think you should. Go wake her up. I can guarantee she won't mind," Free smiled so big I couldn't help but smile back.

After Imani finished her bottle, I handed her to Free and the two of us made our way upstairs to go wake up my baby girl.

When we made it to her room, I stood in the doorway just watching her sleep. She looked so much like her mother that it was scary to me. She was absolutely beautiful, but my baby was far from a baby anymore. She had transformed into a young lady. I looked back at Free, who was waiting patiently in the hallway, and she smiled before she nodded towards my daughter, so I walked in and sat on the bed next to her.

She stirred a little as I pulled her hair out of her face, and for a brief second she opened her eyes and mumbled, "Go away Dey. It's too early."

I chuckled a little before I spoke. "It's not Diego, baby girl. Wake up." I leaned down and kissed her cheek, and she finally opened her eyes and really looked at me. She sat up and tears rolled out of her eyes.

"Dad," she whispered so low that I could barely hear her, but I nodded and pulled her into my arms and hugged her tightly. She hugged me back and wouldn't even let go when I tried to pull away to see her beautiful face. For years, I dreamed about having my baby girl in my arms again, but not once did I believe that it was going to be possible. I guess things have a way of working themselves out, because I was finally home-right where I belonged.

Royal

"Wake yo ass up and get dressed!"

"Why the hell are you yelling in my fuckin ear King, damn? It's too early for that shit, bruh."

"Royal, get yo ass up and get dressed. I need you to make a run with me."

"Fuck King, call Shine's bitch ass. I know Meka got him stressed the fuck out about that damn baby, so I know he's dying to get out the house."

"No muthafucker. This is something you need to handle, so get yo ass up and I'm not gonna ask you again. I'll be there in an hour."

King's ass hung up on me so I rolled over, grabbed my pillow, and coved my head before I yelled, "Fuck!"

Lace snatched the pillow off my head and looked at me like I was crazy. "Why are you yelling like you don't have any damn sense?" she asked.

"I'm tired as fuck and King needs me to make a run with him, now get out of my damn face with all that shit wrapped around your head. I'm already pissed and you're making that shit worse.

Lace's retarded ass nailed me right in my damn chest hard as hell, and it caught me off guard, so it damn near took my breath away.

"The fuck is your problem, damn. You're gonna make me choke your little ass Lace if you keep fucking with me. It's too early for that shit."

"Then your bipolar ass needs to act like you've got some damn sense and stop talking to me like you're damn stupid."

I sat up and grabbed her little ass round the waist, pulling her closer to me before I covered her body with mine. I pinned her arms above her head and narrowed my eyes at her.

"Calm your little ass down before I fuck you up."

"I hate your stupid ass. I swear," she yelled, making me laugh.

"You hate me, Lace?" a smile spread across my face. "You didn't hate me last night, did you?"

"Hmp, I hated our ass last night too, I just tolerate certain parts of you," she mumbled.

"So you hate me but you tolerate my dick?"

"Yep."

"Yeah alright, we'll see about that. You better be glad I got somewhere to go." I let her go and climbed out of bed, but her hard-headed ass threw a pillow at me. I just turned around and mugged her hard as hell before I walked into the bathroom and slammed the door.

I loved the fuck out of her little ass, but I swear on everything that sometimes I felt like I could choke the life out of her. She was so damn stubborn it didn't make any sense. It made me laugh just thinking about it.

I turned on the shower to let the water run hot while I took a piss, and then stepped out of my boxers to get in. The second I closed the glass door, closed my eyes and stepped under the water, I felt a cool breeze and then felt Lace's arms around my waist as she pressed her chest against my back.

"Nah, get the fuck out. You hate me remember?" I looked down over my shoulder at her, and she had a big ass grin on her face as she grabbed my dick and started stroking it.

"You want me to get out?" she asked

"Hell yeah," I said.

She pretended like she was going to open the door, but I knew better. I lifted her short ass and she wrapped her legs around my waist, and the second I pressed her back against the wall, I slide inside her. She bit down on my shoulder hard as hell as I slammed inside of her as rough as possible, until we both came hard as fuck. I held her in place long enough for both of us to catch our breath, and then slowly lowered her to the floor.

She just looked at me and smiled as she reached for her body wash. I just shook my head as we both washed up and got out.

"Where are you going anyway?" Lace asked as sat on the edge of the bed, putting lotion on while I watched her through the mirror.

"The hell if I know. He didn't say."

"I'm going to my mom's house later. I want you to go with me."

"Aight, I hope this shit don't take all day."

"Just call me and let me know if you're gonna be late, and then you can just meet me there."

"Is your brother gonna be there?"

"I don't know, why?" Lace gave me a strange look.

"You know his ass don't like me because his girl always be in my face and shit. You know she's trying to fuck."

"You always think somebody wants your yellow ass, I swear," Lace rolled her eyes, and then walked over to the dresser. She was looking good as hell in her black bra and matching thong; I could feel my soldier rising again.

"I'm telling you Lace, she wants me to fuck her and I'm only telling you because I don't want her ass to corner me while we're there, and then you be mad at me and shit." Lace pulled out a pair of leggings and wiggled into them before she pulled a ribbed tank top over her head, and down around her waist.

"First of all, if she corners your ass you better punch that bitch in the face, because if you don't I'm punching you in the damn face. Second of all, as long as you keep your dick in your pants, then we're good."

She tried to walk off, but I grabbed her feisty ass around the waist and pulled her body into mine before I grabbed her between her legs.

"The only time my dick comes out of my pants is if I'm about to be up in this shit right here, or if a brotha gotta take a piss, so you don't need to worry about that."

"Yeah, well you better keep it that way," she said, and pulled away from me just as I heard my alarm go off, followed by King's voice.

"I hope you're ready to go, muthafucker."

I walked out our bedroom, down the hall to the front door, and didn't see King until he walked out the kitchen with a bottle of water.

"Remind me to change my damn security code."

"Oh, so that's how we're doing it? You walk your ass up in my shit all the damn time," King said before he turned up the bottle of water he had.

"Yeah, but I don't be all in your damn refrigerator and shit," I said with a grin, because I was lying like hell.

"The hell you don't. What's up Lace?" King walked up to Lace and gave her a hug.

"Don't keep him all day, King. I need him to go to my mom's house later," Lace said after she let me go and then walked into the kitchen. I just shook my head at her little demanding ass.

"I'm gone, Lace," I yelled, but she didn't say anything so King and I walked out the front door.

"Where we heading anyway?"

"The mall," Kings said as he walked to the driver side of his truck, but I stopped dead in my tracks.

"I know your ass didn't wake me up to go to the damn mall. The fuck wrong with you?" I yelled, mugging him hard as hell.

"Just get in the damn truck," King said.

"King, you're gon' make me fuck you up, on everything." I was so caught up yelling at King's dumb ass that I didn't even realize somebody was already sitting in the passenger side of his truck until I had the door open.

"I see you haven't changed much," AK said with a big ass grin as he stepped out of King's truck. I looked at King, and then back to AK before I laughed and gave him a hug.

"Please tell me your ass didn't break out of prison," I said when I released AK.

He just chuckled and stared at me. "Nah, I walked out. I'm officially a free man."

"How the fuck did that shit happen?" I asked.

"We'll talk about it later. Just get in the truck so that I can go get my ass some damn clothes."

Same old AK, I thought. I climbed into the back seat, while AK and King got in the front. I couldn't believe this shit, but I was happy as hell. AK was the closest thing I had to a father after my dad was killed, and even before then he always treated me like a son. King and I had basically been brothers since the day we both took our first breaths, and even though we didn't share the same blood, we were family. AK was my father, and I was glad to see his ass outside those cinder block walls. I damn sure never expected to see that shit happen, but here we were and life was good.

*****

"Royal, I made your favorite." Lace's mom threw the towel she was holding over her shoulder as I walked out to her and gave her a hug. Other than their height and mouths, Lace and her mother had nothing in common. Lace basically looked exactly like her dad. Lace's mom was more my complexion with freckles, while Lace was more of a Hershey complexion. Her mom was fine as hell though, because she stayed in the gym doing yoga and shit.

"Word, that's what's up," I said with a grin.

"I'm your child, you need to be making my favorite," Lace frowned at her mother. Lace's mom loved me, and that shit drove Lace crazy because her mom always took my side, especially when the subject of kids came up. She wanted grandkids like yesterday, and since Lace's brother was never with any one female longer than a hot minute, she was on us to make that happen.

"I love you too but, you know Royal is my sweetness."

"That's right ma, tell her what's up." I kissed Lace's mom on the cheek, which made her roll her eyes at both of us hard as hell.

"Besides Shilace, I would make you whatever you wanted if you would stop denying me a grandchild."

"Ma, really?" Lace looked at her mother like she was crazy before she shot me a nasty look.

"Don't Ma me. Royal already made it clear that he's ready. You're already twenty-four Shilace; you don't want to be too old to enjoy your child. Look at me. I'm still young and fine, and you and your brother are grown," She winked at Lace and, then went back to finishing the food she was preparing.

"You heard Ma Lace, you don't want to be too old to enjoy your child," I said with a grin.

"Kiss my ass Royal, I don't want to be tied to your crazy behind for life, so both of you can kill that."

"Keep it up and he's going to walk away and give you what you keep asking for, and we all know you don't want that. You love him. Crazy or not," Her mom said without turning around to look at us.

"Both of you get on my nerves." Lace got up and walked out the kitchen, making me laugh.

Lace's mom glanced at Lace as she walked out, but then turned to me. "Royal, you love my daughter right?"

"Come on ma, you already know," I said flashing her a smile.

"Then you better take care of her heart. I know you got her financially, but you better take care of her heart or you'll have to deal with me. Is that understood?" she asked, waving a wooden spoon at me.

I chuckled a little. "Yes ma'am. I got her. I promise you that, because I damn sure don't want to have to deal with you."

She laughed. "Good, now go in there and pamper her spoiled behind. I swear, she acts like such a baby when it comes to you."

I walked into the living room and plopped down on the sofa next to Lace, and propped my feet on the coffee table before letting my hand rest on her thigh. She looked up from the TV and rolled her eyes at me.

"So you're mad now?" I gently squeezed her thigh before I started rubbing it.

"Oh, so you're worried about how I feel now."

She was acting like such a brat that it made me laugh. "Chill with that shit, Lace. I'm always concerned about how you feel."

"I can't tell."

"How the hell are you so tough all the time, but the second we step foot in your mom's crib you turn into a damn brat?" I leaned towards Lace and kissed her on the neck before I put my arm around her shoulder.

"Because she is a damn brat," Lace's brother Josh walked up behind the sofa and mushed Lace in the head; eventually, he was standing in front of us with his girl.

He dapped me up before he sat down in the La-Z-Boy across from us, with his girl Iesha on his lap.

"Shut up Joshua," Lace yelled, and then rolled her eyes at him. "I don't see how you put up with him," she said, now focused on his girl.

"Because I'm irresistible, my stroke is long and my pockets are fat," Josh said, and then kissed his girl on the cheek, but I'll be damned if her ass wasn't looking right at me. I wondered if Lace peeped that shit.

"What you are is rude and disrespectful," Lace said.

"But you love me Shilace," he looked at her with a grin.

Lace and Josh were so caught up in their conversation that neither of them realized that Iesha was basically eye fucking me. It was getting on my damn nerves, so I jumped my ass up fast as hell when Lace's mom came in to let us know that dinner was ready.

We all stood, but I had to take a piss so I kissed Lace and took off down the hall towards the bathroom, while everyone else was en route to the kitchen, or so I thought.

I walked in and felt tension on the other side, and sure enough, Iesha's trifling ass was on the other side. She stepped in, staring at me all crazy and shit.

"You need to take your ass to the kitchen before Lace comes down here and fucks you up," I said, pointing towards the door.

"She won't if you don't tell, and don't act like you don't want a taste." Her retarded ass lifted her dress, exposing a nicely trimmed pussy. She slid her fingers inside her shit and then pulled them out, holding them in front of my face with big ass grin.

"Your ass is trying to get shot, and hell no I don't want that nasty shit. You walking round with no panties on and shit. There's not tellin' what crawled up in your shit. Get the fuck out of here with all that," I said, trying to keep my voice low.

"My pussy is clean, I can guarantee that. Just taste it and see for yourself." She stepped closer to me, and I shoved her ass back.

"Hell no, your ass is crazy. I'm about to call Lace right now, so that she can come whoop your ass. You're not about to get me caught up."

"Fine," she said, and then laughed. "But you're gonna fuck me. I promise you that."

"Bitch you're dumb." She had me so mad I didn't even have to pee anymore. I moved past her, making sure we didn't have any contact, but the second I hit the hall I turned to look at her.

"Stay the fuck away from me, and wash your damn hands before you bring your trifling ass to the table. That's just nasty." I mugged her hard as fuck before I headed towards the kitchen.

"What's wrong with you?" Lace asked after I sat down next to her.

"Nothing," I said, and then kissed her on the cheek.

"Why you looking like you mad at the world then?" She gave me a curious stare.

"I'm Gucci. Damn ma, that fried chicken looking right," I said, trying to avoid Lace's question.

"You know how I do it," her mom said, and winked at me.

An hour later, a brother was full and feeling lovely, even though Iesha's dumb ass kept staring at me all through dinner, grinning and licking her lips and shit. I was just ready to get my ass up out of there and from around her.

After I hugged Lace's mom and we said our goodbyes, Lace headed to my car, and I was on my way until Josh stopped me.

"Yo, Royal. Can I holla at you for a minute?"

"Yeah, what's up?"

"So word on the street is that you guys are doing it big. I was wondering if you could put a nigga on with your team."

I looked at Josh, not really knowing how to answer. I didn't really know him like that. To be honest, I didn't really know shit about him. He and Lace were okay, but it's not like they were real close because she was never really around him.

"I thought you were already doing your thing," I said.

He looked at me with an expression that was hard to read. "Yeah, but I was thinking it was best to just keep it in the family."

"I'll see what I can do," was all I could come up with.

"Aight, good looking out." He gave me a pound and then walked back into the house, while I made my way to my car and got in.

Lace looked at me strange after I pulled off.

"What was that about?" she asked.

"Nothing." I wasn't sure if I needed to tell her about the conversation, so I just kept it to myself.

"Whatever he's asking, just tell him no," she looked at me serious as hell.

I chuckled. "How do you know he asked me anything?"

"Because I know Josh, and he's always trying to find a come up. He's my brother and I love him, but he's not the most responsible or reliable person, so just tell him no. I don't need any bad blood between the two of you, because it will ultimately affect us."

"I hear you," as all I said. I didn't want to make any promises either way.

"I'm serious Royal. I know Josh and he will fuck up. When he does, he'll have to be dealt with and I don't want that on you, so just tell him no. Please." I could tell that it was an issue for her, so I just agreed. At the moment, I didn't know if I meant it or not, but it's what she needed to hear so I went with it.

"Thank you," she smiled and then looked out the window. I focused on the road and just hoped that I could keep my word. I still had plans to check him out to see what he had to offer, but for now, I was letting it go.

Mo

"Mo, can we go get ice cream?" I smiled when Sasha came running in the room and climbed on the bed with me, but I was in the middle of a conversation with my mother, who was not very happy with me.

"Yes, lady bug. Let me finish this call and then we'll go, okay?" she sat there for a few more seconds, playing with the bangles on my arm before I slid them off and handed them to her. Once she had them on her tiny little wrist, she smiled, climbed off the bed, and then skipped out the door.

"So you're playing nanny to his other child now too," my mother said sarcastically.

"I'm not playing nanny. His daughter's here and I spend time with her. A lot of time with her, because I love her like she was my own," I said before I let out a soft sigh.

"But she's not, Monese. She belongs to that other whore he got pregnant," my mother said sharply. "What would everyone think if they saw you parading around town playing mommy to a stripper's child? That is so beneath you."

I swear I loved my mother, but she needed to worry about her own life and stop trying to run mine. In fact, if she spent more time focused on my father instead of worrying about me spending time with Sasha, then maybe my father wouldn't be sleeping around the way he was. My mother was a beautiful woman, but she sometimes had an ugly soul. No man wants a woman that spends more time tearing him down than building him up.

"Mom, I don't really care what anybody thinks. I love Karter and I love his daughter. I'm happy. Can't you just accept that and let it go?"

"You loved Los too. Isn't that what you said but you cheated on him for years with Karter? And now you're pregnant by him and you love him? You don't know what you want, Monese. You need to just get rid of that baby and focus on modeling. I wished I had been smart enough to do that, so I'm trying to make sure you don't make the same mistakes that I made."

My mother had no idea how inconsiderate her statement was. She was basically calling me a mistake while trying to tell me that she had my best interest at heart. She regretted having me. I had heard it all my life, and here she was reminding me again. I ruined her modeling career. I was the reason why she had to marry my father, who apparently was never good enough for her.

"I'm keeping this baby, so you might as well not even bring that up again and yeah I did love Los, but so what? He beat me nearly every day that I was with him, but I was too stupid to leave, even when Karter begged me to. I learned my lesson when he killed mine and Karter's first child. I wasn't going to let that happen again."

"I don't know what to say about you. It's just disappointing, I guess. I really wanted more for you."

"More like what, ma? You've owned me since I was two years old. I did everything you wanted and lived the way you wanted. I'm famous, Ma. I'm a success. You can brag about me to your friends over coffee or tea as you flip through the magazines showing off my print ads. What more do I need to do for you to be happy?"

"You're saying that like I did it for me. It wasn't about me. I invested all that time in your career for you Monese, and it's an insult that you would insinuate that there was any other intent involved. You never complained when you were getting those six figure contracts, now did you?"

"No Ma, you're right, and I appreciate everything that you've ever done for me, but right now I just want to focus on this baby. I'm happy. I love Karter and he loves me, so right now it's about us and our family. Can you respect that?"

"He's a street thug Monese, a typical street thug. How am I supposed to explain that? He might be Liam Davidson's son, but he's nothing like his father. He's just your typical street thug, so how can I explain that?"

"You just did. How about you just tell everyone that he's Liam Davidson's son. I'm sure that will make everyone happy."

"Don't by cute, Monese."

"Ma, I have to go."

"When are you coming to visit? I'm sure your father would love to see you."

I almost laughed. She was so oblivious to how little she cared. My father would love to see me. No mention of how much she wanted to see me. In fact, the only reason she wanted me there was so that she could try to interrogate Karter with the hopes of running him off. That's the main reason why I didn't want to go without him, because I could handle her with him by my side and even if I couldn't, I knew that he could. I missed my father, but to see him I had to see my mother, and I wasn't looking forward to that.

"I'm not sure. Karter is really busy right now, but I'll be sure to let you know."

"Yeah, you do that."

"Good bye Ma.

"I love you, Monese," she said cheerfully, as if someone flipped a switch. This woman was insane.

"I love you too, Ma."

I sat there for a few more minutes, allowing myself time to release the tension surrounding me before I walked into the living room so that I could let Sasha know that we were leaving soon. I found her laid out on the floor surrounded by a coloring book and crayons.

"Hey lady bug, go get your shoes on so that we can get ready to go."

She looked up at me and smiled. "Can I finish this picture for Daddy first?"

"Yep, but then after that get your shoes on. I'm going to go get dressed."

Sasha sat up and crossed her little legs. "Are you wearing your UGGs? If you are, then I'm wearing mine."

She had the biggest grin on her face as she looked up at me.

"Then I'll wear mine and we can be twins."

"Good," she giggled.

She looked so much like Karter that I couldn't help but wonder what our child was going to look like. I couldn't wait. I don't think I have ever loved someone so much in all my life.

After I was dressed in leggings, a sweatshirt, and my UGGs, we grabbed our purses and got in the elevator. Sasha made me find her a sweatshirt that was the same color as mine, and she sported her Coach purse that I had gotten her to match one that I had.

We headed to the mall to get ice-cream and do a little shopping. I loved spending time with Sasha. She was so smart and funny that she kept me entertained. She was definitely her father's child, which made me love her even more. After we did a little shopping, purchasing some matching items, and a quick stop at the nail shop, we settled into the food court for ice cream. Sasha sat across from me making a huge mess while I scrolled through my phone checking messages, until I heard a voice behind me.

"So I guess that bitch thinks she's going to take my place. She will never be a mother to my child, and I'll make sure of that."

"Girl, go get your daughter. That high class hoe won't do shit."

"Nah, I got shit to do today. She better be glad, or else I would embarrass her ass."

I didn't have to turn around to know it was Saria. I laughed, because Karter told me the whole story about why Sasha was staying with us, and how he had to check her, so I knew she wasn't stupid enough to approach me. She didn't want to have to answer to Karter, but if she did I had something for her. I was a model, but I also grew up in Brooklyn, so I didn't have a problem checking a bitch for disrespecting me. Sasha looked up and realized her mother was near, and a frown formed on her face. She pointed to her mother with the look of disappointment.

"I don't have to go with her, do I?" she said softly.

I glanced over my shoulder. "No lady bug, you're staying with me."

Sasha was smiling again. "Good. I want to stay with you. Daddy said that I can live with you now; does that mean that you're going to be my mommy?"

If looks could kill, I would be dropping in a casket. I could see Saria's mouth drop open as she was on her way past us, but stooped dead in her tracks when she heard her daughter.

"No lady bug, she will always be your mother. I'm just somebody who loves you and takes care of you when your mommy doesn't."

"That means you're my mommy," Sasha said with a grin.

"Something like that. Let's go so we can head home to see your dad."

Saria stood there with the look of disappointment; her daughter didn't even acknowledge her, and that was punishment enough for me. I flashed her a smile as I grabbed Sasha's hand and we left her standing there looking stupid. Some shit just worked itself out on its own. I couldn't have planned it better if I had tried.

*****

"Where have you guys been?" Karter asked as soon as I walked into the bedroom. He had just showered, because the smell of his cologne filled the room and he was dressed casually in fleece sweat pants and a V-neck, looking sexy as ever. I could tell that he had just gotten a haircut.

"We went shopping today," Sasha yelled as she ran in the room and hugged Karter's legs. He picked her up and hugged her before he positioned her in one arm; pulling me into a hug with the other. After a quick kiss, he let me go and walked into the living room.

"I see your twinning today," he said, eyeing my outfit and then Sasha's.

"Yep," Sasha giggled.

"What did you buy me?" Karter said after he sat down on the sofa with Sasha on his lap. She turned to face him and frowned.

"We didn't get you anything, but I colored you a picture." She jumped down and ran into her room, returning a few minutes later with a page that she ripped out of her coloring book.

"You made this for me?" Karter said, pretending to be over the top excited. I loved the way he was with her. He was a completely different person. Goofy and free.

"Yep, do you like it?" she asked proudly.

"I love it." He kissed her. "Go hang it on the refrigerator for me."

She darted towards the kitchen and grabbed one of the magnets to hang her picture with, and then ran right back to Karter.

"We saw Mommy at the mall, but Mo said I didn't have to go with her. Daddy, why can't Mo be my mommy now since I live here?"

He looked at me, concerned after hearing that we saw Saria, but then smiled at Sasha. "She is your mommy, because she loves you and she loves me."

"See Mo, I told you you're my mommy."

Karter playfully yanked one of Sasha's ponytails. "Why don't you go color a picture for Mo while we figure out what's for dinner?"

"Okay!" she yelled, and then took off running towards her room again. When she was gone, I sat down next to Karter and he grabbed my hand, lacing his fingers thorough mine.

"What was that all about?" he asked.

"It was nothing. She didn't really say anything to either one of us, but she was talking trash to one of her girls." I didn't really want him to flip out.

"She just can't leave well enough alone. I swear, she's gonna make me fuck her up." Just that fast, he was pissed and had murder in his eyes.

"Just let it go. I'm fine, Sasha's fine, and Saria is irrelevant." I leaned over and kissed him. He looked at me blankly for a minute, but then finally smiled.

"How my baby?" he said, sliding his hand under my sweatshirt.

"Good I guess."

"Did you eat?"

"Yes Karter. We had lunch at the mall and you watched me eat breakfast this morning," I said dryly.

"Please don't start with that. I'm just concerned." He put his arm around me and kissed me on the top of my head.

"I know."

"What do you feel like eating?"

"Doesn't matter, let Sasha choose."

"Hell no. All her little ass wants to eat is Chick-fil-A. I'm not trying to hear that. I need some real food, and I know you already had it at the mall, didn't you?"

"I plead the fifth."

"Exactly," he said, and then laughed

"Do you want me to cook?"

"Nah, you're good. We can order something."

Karter stood up and grabbed the menus out of the kitchen, and we settled in trying to figure out dinner, even though we both knew that one of us would be making a trip to Chick-fil-A before the night was over.

*****

"What's on your mind, Mo?" Karter pulled me into his side and kissed me on my forehead. This was one of the first nights in a longtime that Karter was actually home with us. I always knew when he was on a job, because he would leave early in the morning and crawl in bed with me late at night. I missed him, but I didn't mind because it was who he was, but tonight he was here with me and I was content.

"Nothing." I kissed his chest before I positioned my head on it and let my hand slid across his abs.

"Come on Mo, I know you. I can hear you thinking."

"How can you hear me thinking," I laughed.

"Your ass is so deep in thought that I can hear that shit, so just tell me."

"I talked to my mom today." Karter didn't say anything, but he didn't have to; I knew what he was thinking.

"How did that go?" he finally said after a few minutes.

"Same as always," I said. I felt his chest rise and then fall before he pulled away from me and positioned his body over mine, being careful not to let all of his weight fall on me.

"Look, I know you love your mom, but she be on some shit, Mo. Don't let her stress you out. It's not good for you or the baby."

"I know, she just makes it hard."

"Try not to worry about it." Karter started kissing me on my neck.

"I miss my dad."

Karter lifted his head and stared at me for a few seconds before he started kissing my neck again. He eventually sat up on his knees and pulled me to a seated positioned before he lifted my shirt and pulled it over my head.

"Then we'll go see him," he said as he lowered his body on top of mine again, and began kissing my stomach.

"Are you sure?" I let my hands go across his head as he made is way in between my legs. Karter lifted his head as his slide h0is fingers inside me.

"If it's what you want, then we'll go."

Karter lowered his head again and when I felt his tongue, I knew he was done talking. I closed my eyes and let everything else go. He was all that mattered right now.

Free

"Aye boo, are you on your way?" I asked as soon as Lace answered.

"I just pulled up."

I walked to the front door with Mani in my arms, and pulled it open just as Lace hit the steps. As soon as she was within reach, she took Mani out of my arms, kissed me on the cheek, and then walked past me into the house.

"What time is everybody supposed to be here?" Lace asked as we entered the kitchen. There was stuff everywhere, and the caterers were moving around like they owned the place.

"Seven, I think," I said as I grabbed two bottles of water, and then headed towards the living room.

I looked around our house, and there was stuff everywhere. Dey insisted on getting the crew together to throw a dinner in honor of his dad coming home. Since our clique had damn near doubled in size, Dey told me to hire caterers to handle the food. I was glad, because I definitely wasn't in the mood to cook for that many people.

"So why the hell were you rushing me over here if you're not doing anything?" Lace asked as she alternated between frowning at me and smiling at Mani.

"Because I was bored and didn't want to sit her by myself all day. I couldn't leave, because you know Dey will lose his mind if I leave all these people in here alone.

"So you called me over here to babysit you," Lace said with a grin.

"Shut up hoe, I called you over here to be a good best friend and keep my company."

"Same thing boo," Lace said as she leaned down until she and Mani were face to face. Mani started laughing, making Lace laugh.

"It doesn't matter. I'm just glad you're here."

"So he's legit free, no chance on going back?" Lace asked, now focused on me.

"From what Dey says, yes."

"So is he getting back in the business?"

"Nope, I asked Dey the same thing and he said his dad told him that he was done. He had plenty of money and there was no reason for him to. He said he was a free man and planned on staying that way."

"Oh my God, have you talked to Meka today?" Lace all but yelled.

"No why?"

"Guess who's coming with them tonight?" Lace said, looking at me like she was about to explode waiting for me to respond.

"I don't know, just tell me."

"Sky," Lace said, keeping her eyes glued to me waiting for my reaction.

"Shut up," I yelled "you're kidding right?"

"Nope, this was the first time that she was supposed to stay overnight at their house, and Shine wasn't going to come tonight, but she told him he had to, so he's bringing the baby.

I felt a little torn. I had a certain loyalty to Meka, but I wanted to see the baby. Even though Meka was trying to deal with the whole situation, I knew it was still messing with her. Shine had been spending time with Sky, but Asia would drop her off at his mom's house and he would go see her there. Meka was always with him, but she didn't really interact with her much because Shine and his mom usually handled her. Every time I talked to her about it, she pretended like she was cool with it, but it had to be hard.

I was just ready for her baby to get here, because I knew that would make things a lot easier. Right now, Meka felt like her baby wasn't as important because he wasn't here yet, even though Stanly was working overtime to make her think anything but. I actually believed that he had gotten his shit together the way he was going all in trying to make things up with Meka, but that baby was a constant reminder. It made it impossible for Meka to forget.

I wanted to see the baby because after the way everyone fell in love with Mani, I thought for sure we would all love Sky. I mean, after all, she was still Shine's daughter and we love him, but every time I thought about it I felt guilty, like I was betraying Meka.

"I kind of can't wait to see her," I said, feeling guilty for saying it out loud.

"Girl me too. Is that bad? Are we bad friends?" Lace asked.

"I don't know. I mean, Meka keeps saying she fine, but I still feel like we shouldn't want anything to do with the baby, out of respect for her."

"Yeah I know, but then it's not really fair to Shine. It is his daughter."

"Oh my God, I hate complications!" I yelled, and then fell back into the sofa.

"I know boo, but I guess we'll just have to see how it goes tonight."

"So what's going on with you lately? You've been spending so much time with Royal that I feel like I never get to see you anymore."

"Dang boo, if I didn't know any better I'd say you sound jealous, Free."

"Maybe I am. He stole you from me and I miss you," I gave Lace a pitiful look, causing her to laugh at me.

"I'm always your boo. You had me first. He just gets sloppy seconds."

"Oh, so I'm get Free's sloppy seconds," Royal said as he stood in the hallway outside the living room.

"How did you get in here?" Lace asked, frowning at him.

"The front door, but answer my question Lace."

"Why didn't I hear the alarm?" she said, looking at me.

"I turned it off because the caterers kept going in and out and it was driving me crazy, now answer your man boo," I said with a grin.

She glanced at me like she could murder me, and then looked at Royal. "Technically yes. She had me first so you are getting her leftovers," Lace said.

"Damn Free, I didn't know you got down like that. King know that shit?" Royal said with a grin.

"You're so damn stupid, I swear. You know what we mean," Lace said.

"I'm just fucking with you, chill."

Royal walked into the living room and took Mani from Lace. "Let me see this fat ass baby," he said after he had her securely in his arms.

"You better stop calling my baby fat, Royal."

"Why, she is," he said as he started making faces at her. "You know Shine's bringing his outside child tonight."

I looked at him and laughed. "Dang Royal, you gossip more than we do. Should I call you next time we're having a girl's night?"

"Fuck you, Free. I'm not gossiping. I'm just stating facts. Shit, his ass called and told me, and now I'm telling you. How the fuck is that gossiping?" he tried to keep a straight face when he looked at me, but ended up laughing.

"It just is and you know it," I said.

"Blame her little ass. Always got me watching Lifetime and Basketball Wives and shit like that."

"Don't front for Free. You're the one who records that stuff," Lace said with a grin.

"Hell yeah, cause if I don't your little ass be going in on me."

"Whatever man."

"Free, did Lace tell you the good news?"

I looked at Lace with a curious stare just as Dey walked in and took Mani from Royal.

"What's up, what we talking about?" he asked.

"Apparently Royal and Lace have some good news," I said

"Word, what's up Lace?"

"Hell I don't know. I guess it's news to me too," Lace said as she looked at Royal, confused.

"We're having a baby?" Royal said, smiling like a little kid.

"You're pregnant?" I said, and looked right at Lace.

"Hell no. I don't know what that idiot is talking about," she yelled, and then looked at Royal, along with me and Dey.

His stupid self just laughed. "But we're trying though," Royal said.

"Uh no boo. We're not," Lace said.

"Yes hell we are. We talked about this."

"You said you wanted a baby, and I said I would think about it. That's not working on it, smart ass," Lace said, and rolled her eyes at Royal.

"You're stupid as fuck man," Dey shook his head and laughed.

"What's the difference?"

"There's a big difference. I said I'd think about it. I didn't agree to anything," Lace said.

"Don't make me call Susan," Royal said.

"Dang Lace, he pulled the mother card on you." Now I was laughing.

"Wait, so your mother is on team baby?" Dey asked.

"She's on team anything, as long as his crazy ass agrees to it."

"Damn that's fucked up. I didn't think anybody liked his yellow ass," Dey said

"Fuck you King, everybody love me."

"Not even close," Lace said.

I just shook my head and listened to the two of them going back and forth. I swear, they were meant for each other because no one else in their right mind would put up with either one of them.

*****

It was just after 8:00, and everyone was already at the house expect Shine and Meka. She had just called telling me that they got caught up at Shine's mother's house, but they were almost there.

"Was that Meka?" Lane asked after I ended the call.

All the girls were sitting in the kitchen talking while all the guys were in the theater room watching a game. Well, all the girls expect Mira. She was wherever her dad was, and had been that way since he stepped foot in the house. It was cute to see them together, but I think it made Dey a little jealous. For the past ten years, it had been just the two of them, but now that his dad was home, it was like he was being pushed to the side. I knew he understood, but it still didn't make it hurt any less.

"Yeah, she said they'll be here in a minute," I said.

"Do they have the baby?" Mo asked, and all eyes were on me waiting for the answer.

"She didn't say, but I guess so since she said the got caught up at his mom's house. That's where they usually meet to get her."

"Is it weird that I can't wait see the baby?" Lane asked.

Lace and I looked at each other. "Nah, we're the same way," I said.

"Me too, but I kind of feel bad. I just love babies though," Mo said.

"You think you do. Just wait until that one gets here," I said, pointing at her stomach. "Hanging out with Sasha and dealing with a newborn are two completely different things, just wait," I said.

"Girl please. Mani is the best baby in the world. She never cries and she was sleeping through the night when she was two weeks old, so shut up," Lane said.

"But she's still a lot of work," I said.

"I'll probably have some demon child that cries all the time and never sleeps," Mo said

"Nah, that will be Lace," Lane said, and then laughed.

"Don't jinx me like that," Lace balled up her napkin and threw it at Lane, "but you're right though. We all know Royal has bad blood."

"That's cold, Lace," I said.

"Damn Free, chill, I didn't mean it like that. I'm talking about him, not his crazy family," Lace said, and then laughed.

"Front door open."

We all looked at each other and jumped up. Everyone was there except Meka and Shine, so it had to be them. We all made our way to the foyer and sure enough, they were both standing there. Shine had the baby carrier while Meka stood next to him. She was due in the next two weeks, so she looked like she was about to explode, but she was smiling.

We must have all been thinking the same thing, because neither of us wanted to be obvious, so we went straight to Meka and hugged her first; we all spoke to Shine, but none of us addressed the baby.

"You can see her," Meka said, killing the awkwardness that surrounded us. I guess we were a little too obvious.

"Are you sure?" I asked, looking Meka right into her eyes.

She smiled and turned to Shine. "Bring her in the kitchen and I got her. I know the guys are waiting for you."

We all followed Shine into the kitchen, and he sat the carrier down on the island, kissed Meka, and then rubbed her stomach.

"They're in the theater room," I said, and then he left us and went to join the guys.

"Can I hold her?" Lane asked.

"Yes, you can hold her," Meka said with a grin.

"So I guess things are better now?" I asked Meka, while everyone else focused on the baby, who Lane now had in her arms.

"It's not perfect, but look at her. She's just a baby, how can I be mad at her?" Meka said, turning to look at Sky, "Now don't get me wrong, I hate her damn mother and as soon as I drop this load I'm whooping her ass, but that baby didn't ask to be here."

"Your dumb Meka, but I'm helping you beat that hoe," Lace said.

"Girl me too, count me in," Mo said.

"Damn Mo, it's like that? I didn't know you rocked like that," Lace said.

"I'm a Brooklyn girl. Don't let the labels fool you," Mo said, serous as hell.

"Are you sure this is Shine's baby? She don't look anything like him," Lane said.

"That's what the test said, but he claims he was saving it all for our Zion," Meka said, rubbing her stomach.

"I guess so, because I don't see any of him in this baby," Lace said, now focused on Sky. "She's cute though–wait, can I say that?" Lace's stupid self looked at Meka and frowned.

"Girl you're dumb," Meka said.

An hour later, I was standing in the living room with Dey, who was behind me with his arms wrapped around my waist. Royal was on the sofa next to AK with Lace on his lap, while Karter and Kay were standing in front of him, deep in conversation about something. Meka was on Shine's lap in a leather chair that sat in the corner, while he had his arms around her, rubbing her stomach with Sky in her carrier at his feet.

Meka

I woke up with the worst pain ever, and it came out of nowhere. It was so strong it took my breath away. I grabbed Shine's arm causing, him to jump up and look at me.

"What's wrong?" he said the second he looked at me.

"I think I just had a contraction," I said.

"Okay, hang on." He climbed out of bed, turned the light on, and started grabbing clothes.

"What are you doing?" I asked, looking at him strange.

"You just said you had a contraction. We need to go to the hospital, right?"

"No--"

Before I could finish what I was saying, another one hit me and it was equally painful so I closed my eyes, balled up my fist trying, and tried to ease the pain. The second I opened my eyes again, Shine was in his jeans staring at me.

"Meek, get up. I think you're in labor," Shine said, looking worried.

"It doesn't happen that fast," I said.

"Dr. Mitchell said that sometimes first babies come fast, Meek. You can't have this baby here so get up and—" He stopped talking when the second another contraction hit me, and when I opened my eyes again, he was next to me.

"Let's go." He reached for my hand and didn't move until I took it and got up.

"I'm not going to the hospital yet, Stanly."

"Meek I'm not playing, get dressed. We're going to the hospital, and if they want to send us home then that's fine, but we're going."

I just rolled my eyes at him and got dressed. I knew that I was having contractions, but I didn't believe that I was actually in labor yet. My water hadn't broke yet, and I kind of actually felt normal until the contractions hit.

An hour later, I was in a hospital bed and hooked to monitors, while Stanly paced the floor asking me how I was doing every five minutes.

"Will you sit down? You're driving me crazy with all that," I said, waving my hand towards him just as another contraction hit.

I closed my eyes and clenched my fist until it passed. Free told me that they hurt like hell, but she didn't say it was like your body was being ripped apart.

"Hell, your ass is driving me crazy with all that. You're too damn calm to be in labor. That shit is not normal."

"And you know this how? You've never done this before either," I rolled my eyes at him.

"I was there when Reesey was born, and trust me when I say my mother was not this calm. In fact, they had to give her all kinds of shit just to keep her calm."

"Everybody is different Stanly. Just Chill I'm—"

Again, another contraction hit and it was a little stronger than the others, but I was fine as soon as it passed.

"Something is seriously wrong with you. I swear, this shit is not normal, Meek."

I looked at him and laughed. "What do you want me to do, yell and scream and act crazy?"

"Do something, shit." He looked at me like I was crazy. I could tell that he was nervous and stressed, but I needed him to calm all that down. Hell, there wasn't any room for me to get crazy because he was doing it for me. He had all that covered right now, but I had to admit it was mildly cute but more annoying.

"Do I need to call the nurse and ask them to bring you something? Apparently you need drugs more than I do."

He just laughed. "All I need as a damn blunt right now and I'll be straight, but I know I can't smoke that shit in here."

I just looked at him and shook my head. He was serious as hell, which was funny to me. If this baby didn't come soon, he was going to lose it. A few minutes later, someone knocked on the door just before it opened.

"How are we doing Tameka?" a tall, thin, blond woman stepped in room holding a clipboard. She smiled at me and then Stanly.

"It's Meka," I said, eyeing her.

"Who the fuck are you?" Shine asked.

"Stanly!" I yelled, letting him know that I wasn't happy. I swear, he thought they could talk to people any kind of way.

She smiled. "It's fine. This is a stressful situation, and I understand that. I'm Dr. Lewis. Dr. Mitchell is out of town, and I'm on rotation today, so I'll be delivering your baby."

"Um okay," I said, not really thrilled about Dr. Mitchell not being here. I made eye contact with Shine to make sure he didn't say anything stupid.

"Trust me, I know you would prefer to have Dr. Mitchell here, but I promise you you're in good hands. Do you mind if I take a look to see where we are?"

"No that's fine," I said just before another contraction hit. Dr. Lewis waited for it to pass before she checked my cervix and informed us that I was about six centimes dilated. Since my water had yet to break, she decided that it needed to be manually done and told us that it shouldn't be long, based on my contractions and how fast I was dilating. I smiled, nodded, and the second she was out the room, I looked at Stanly.

"Call everybody," I said.

"Meek, it's five in the morning. I'm not about to wake everybody up." He looked at me like I was crazy.

"And I'm not about to have this baby without my girls here. That's not happening, and they would kill me if I did."

"Meek, really?"

"Either you call them or I will."

Another contraction hit and after it passed, I focused on Shine again, who was just watching me.

"I'm in labor with your son. Are you really not going to do the one thing I asked you to do?"

He looked at me and let out a long sigh before he made his first call. I smiled and waited. I guess there was some benefits to being him labor. As another contraction hit, I closed my eyes and waited for it to pass. I loved my son, but I needed him to hurry up and get here. I was over this part already.

Three hours later, I was completely drained and holding my son. I looked down at his tiny little face, amazed at how much I loved him already. I couldn't believe that he was finally in my arms, and I didn't want to let him go.

"Can I hold my son?" I shook my head without even looking up at Shine. I wasn't ready to let Zion go.

"Meek. Let me hold him." He kissed me on my forehead and tucked a few lose strands of my hair behind my ear.

"Can we finally see him?" Free said as she walked in, with King behind her carrying Imani in her car seat. She was wide awake and smiling.

"Good luck with that. I can't even see him," Shine said as King walked up to him and gave him a hug.

"Congrats man."

"Preciate it."

"It took them long enough to get you in here. I mean dang," Lace said as she walked in with Royal. Karter and Mo were right behind them. I laughed thinking about all of them waiting for me to get into my room.

"I know right," Mo said. Everyone was hovering, but I still wasn't ready to let Zion go."

"Alright hoe, stop hogging him. His auntie wants to see him," Lace said.

"Oh hell no. Not until I hold him," Shine said.

I kissed Zion on his forehead and then handed him to Shine. Royal was next to him, and of course he had to say something crazy.

"Damn Shine, he looks just like your ugly ass."

"Fuck you Royal," Shine said just as Lace punched Royal in the arm.

"I swear, something is wrong with you. I need to find out what floor they do testing on, because I'm taking your stupid ass up there," she said.

"You better chill the fuck out before Lace fucks around and gets you committed," King said, and we all looked at Royal and laughed.

"Committed for what?" Lane asked as soon as she walked in the room with Kay.

"Because he's crazy," Lace said.

"Just because I say what everybody else is thinking doesn't mean I'm crazy. It just means I'm honest," Royal said.

"Nah, your ass is just rude," Karter said.

"Let me hold him, Stanly," Free said with a grin.

"Hell no, I told you about calling me that," Shine said, and turned his back to Free.

"That's your name, Stanly," Free said, putting emphasis on Stanly.

"Let her hold him," I said.

"Oh, so your ass didn't want to even let me hold my son, now you're trying to make me give him to Free?"

"Uh yeah," I said with a grin.

"I swear, we can't win for shit," King said.

"That's your problem. It's not always about winning," Free said, and reached for Zion but this time Shine let him go. Once she had him securely in her arms, Lace, Lane, and Mo surrounded her waiting their chance to hold him.

I was tired and I felt like I had been hit by a truck, but I was happy that my crew was here. I knew that Zion was going to be loved.

"Can I have my son please?" I looked at Lace, who currently had Zion. Royal was standing behind her looking over her shoulder at him while they were whispering and grinning. Something was up with the two of them.

"So you want to be all selfish with him," Lace said with a smirk before she walked over and handed him to me.

"I just miss my little man," I said as I looked down at him and smiled. He was wide awake and looking right at me. He kept puckering his little lips, which was the most adorable thing I had ever seen. I was so in love with him.

"I know those nurses are out there bugging and shit, because we got like twenty people in her," Kay said, looking around at everyone.

"Man I don't give a fuck. With all that money they charge, they should be bringing all of us breakfast and shit," Shine said.

"You're dumb bruh, but you're right though. They're making a killing off this shit," King said.

"They're making a killing off of us," Karter said. "First King and Free, now Shine and Meka, and then me and Mo. That's a hundred grand right there. I'm starting to think Royal was right. We should have asked for the group discount. Fifty percent off on your next baby."

"Damn Karter, that's what's up," Kay said.

"Y'all need to make that shit happen; who's next?" Shine said.

"Are you gonna tell them or am I?" Royal said with a big ass grin. I knew something was up with the two of them.

"Oh my God, you just can't keep your mouth closed for shit," Lace said, and then punched Royal in the chest.

All eyes were on her, and she rolled her eyes and let out a long sigh.

"Fine, we're pregnant," Lace said like she was annoyed about it, which made me laugh.

We all looked at each other, and I swear we all basically had the same reaction, but Free was the first to speak.

"It's about damn time," she said.

"The fuck you mean *WE*? Your ass is pregnant. I just made that shit happen," Royal said with a smirk.

"Nah, that's not how it works dumb ass. *WE* are pregnant. We're doing this together. You wanted it, now you've got it so get ready," Lace snapped.

"Damn Royal, I think you just fucked up bruh," King said.

"We need our own reality show. This is about to be too much, I swear," Lane said.

"Man fuck that. You're trying to get all of us put up under the jail. You know how we roll," Royal said.

"Not that part of our lives, dummy."

"Shit I'm just saying. I'm too pretty to be up in somebody's jail," Royal said.

"I can't even deal with you. I swear," Lace said, and then rolled her eyes.

I couldn't help but smile. Royal and Lace were already beyond dysfunctional, so adding a baby to that mix was definitely going to be interesting. I couldn't wait to see how this was going play out....

COMING SOON:

A Criminal Love: Royal and Lace

Join our mailing list to get a notification when Leo Sullivan Presents has another release!

Text LEOSULLIVAN to 22828

to join!

Latest release

The Cocaine Princess 6

Check out our upcoming releases on the next page!

To submit a manuscript for our review, email us at leosullivanpresents@gmail.com

CPSIA information can be obtained
at www.ICGtesting.com
Printed in the USA
LVOW04s1738021216
515533LV00009B/569/P